MAMA RAISED A KILLER

PART II

-

THE REVENGE

MAMA RAISED A KILLER

PART II

-

THE REVENGE

BY MARK SAINT CYR

MARK SAINT CYR

COPYRIGHT © 2010 BY MARK SAINT CYR.

LIBRARY OF CONGRESS CONTROL NUMBER:
0982748213

ISBN: 978 0 9827 4821 3

ALL RIGHTS RESERVED. NO PART OF THIS BOOK MAY BE REPRODUCED OR TRANSMITTED IN ANY FORM OR BY ANY MEANS, ELECTRONIC OR MECHANICAL, INCLUDING PHOTOCOPYING, RECORDING, OR BY ANY INFORMATION STORAGE AND RETRIEVAL SYSTEM, WITHOUT PERMISSION IN WRITING FROM THE COPYRIGHT OWNER.

THIS IS A WORK OF FICTION. NAMES, CHARACTERS, PLACES AND INCIDENTS EITHER ARE THE PRODUCT OF THE AUTHOR'S IMAGINATION OR ARE USED FICTITIOUSLY, AND ANY RESEMBLANCE TO ANY ACTUAL PERSONS, LIVING OR DEAD, EVENTS, OR LOCALES IS ENTIRELY COINCIDENTAL.

THIS BOOK WAS PRINTED IN THE UNITED STATES OF AMERICA.

To order additional copies of this book, contact:

ATG TECHNOLOGIES & PUBLISHING

P O BOX 40422

REDFORD, MICHIGAN 48240

atgsmith@att.net

mrkii@att.net

and visit our social web-site

atgcentral.com

a division of
Atg Technologies and Filmworks,LLC

ACKNOWLEDGEMENTS:

I GIVE PRAISE TO THE LORD ALMIGHTY JESUS CHRIST, WHO SHOWED ME THE RIGHT PATH TO ACHIEVE MY GOALS. AS ALWAYS I THANK MY DECEASED PARENTS ETHEL JEANETTE SMITH AND DOUGLAS LEE SMITH FOR NEUTERING MY IDEAS. I JUST WISH YOU WERE HERE TO EXPERIENCE THIS WITH ME. TO MY LIFELONG PARTNER FOR LOVING ME AND HELPING ME THROUGH THE ROUGH TIMES, I LOVE YOU MUCH. TO ALL FAMILY, FRIENDS AND FANS, THANKS FOR THE SUPPORT. IF WE ALL SUPPORTED EACH OTHER WE ALL AS A RACE WILL STRIDE IN THE RIGHT DIRECTION.

Mark Saint Cyr

Mama Raised A Killer II

Chapter 1   The Gucci's Revenge

I stood in the background and watched the hundreds of people paying their respects. I didn't know my life had reached so many people. I watched as the tears flowed from friends and the constant hugs Mama received. I got the notion to cry myself for seeing such an out pour of love coming from a community that hated what I did. When the hearse stopped at the burnt down pool hall my mind drifted to my last time there. I had just sold the pool hall and was reminiscing about the good times we had there. Cye, mama and I had so many memories. I was standing in the empty pool hall when the doors burst open and caught me off guard as two white men stepped in the hall shooting guns and one man threw a lighted flame bottle filled with liquid. I was hit by a bullet as I fled for the office and passed out for a minute. I woke up smelling smoke. I was trapped. My mind was fading in and out. The smoke entered my lungs and I was caught between life and death. Caught between the smoke filling my lungs pulling life out of me and between all the dead people I had killed directly or indirectly. That were smiling and motioning me, taunting me to come join them. I saw Carl my ex boyfriend who died in my arms trying to protect me, guns blazing but no one was falling. The last thing I remember before passing out was seeing Satan himself personally give me an invitation to hell, picking me up in his arms. I coughed for a while and thought satin was breathing in my mouth pulling me into the incinerator of fire with his hot breath. I struggled to catch some air and my mind started to focus. Satin in his red suit was Reggie. Carl's cousin, he had on a red shirt. He saw my car when the pool hall was on fire and came in to recue me. He was giving me mouth to mouth. The fire man took over then I passed out and woke up in the hospital. I had been shot in my side. The bullet went in and out. When I got out of the hospital, Cye,

Mama Raised A Killer II

mama and I decided that we should continue with the story that I died in the blaze. So here I sit, mourning over a casket that is supposed to have me in it. At the church the preacher hit home be talking about selling drugs and how drugs was Killing our community. He talked good about me and how I tried to help the people in the neighborhood, by loaning money to those in need. Mama must have paid him good for the kind words he spoke about me. I was beginning to believe his words myself. Then shots rang out. People were screaming, and guys were shooting back. I ducked in an aisle and the next thing I knew I was being trampled. The emergency exit was where I was hiding. I felt my arm being pulled it was mama she was pulling me up to leave. We all went out the side door, where two men ran passed us with their guns out. While mama and I walked back to the car we talked about our need to escape from the North End, our way out of the drugs, violence, death, and the envy you receive from people when you have the power that being a drug dealer gives you.

3

Mark Saint Cyr

That night we left town on our way to California. Hoping to change our life's forever. Uncle DC and Aunt Keysha, Cye's parents gave us directions from the airport. The day was beautiful. It was about 2:30 the sun was shining and the warm autumn air was blowing slightly. The smell in the air was unlike the smell of the North End. The poverty, the death and destruction was not evident in the air out here in California. The smell and the people made me realize what I been missing in my life. I thought I was on top of the world, above most people in the old neighborhood I had money and the power to control people's life's. In California everybody has money. I'm just a person, I'm looked at like everyone else with no hang up's. No one knows me or my past. I can finally put my gun down and start carrying a small purse. Mama and I got settled in at Cye's house. A beautiful house off the beach, with a terrace that you can sit and watch the sun rise and listen to the waves beat against the marina while the boats shay back and forth in the distance. It was so pleasant and serene. I woke up every morning at 6:AM to catch the sun rise. I had Carl's child in April a beautiful 8 pound four ounce baby girl. I named her Carletha after Carl. She looked just like him and I vowed to keep her away from the fast life. This was a good time in my life for me. It was the first time since my daddy was alive that I felt secure. I was away from the fast life. I just enjoyed being with family Cye, Mama, Uncle DC, and aunt Keysha where inseparatable. Raising Carletha was a full time job and I didn't Have time to even think about a man. I was really happy. It was Carletha's third birthday and we were having a party. Cye, and I went to the mall to pick up a cake and some gold earrings. I wanted to have her ears pierced. I remember looking at my watch and got a little dizzy. "Wants wrong, Tee?" Cye asked. I don't know I feel a little dizzy' I said. "You, ok" as she grabbed my arm. "It's one o'clock, we got to get home the party starts at four" I managed to say. "Girl, you look sick. But you can't be pregnant you ain't had a man since you been in California." She said and started laughing. "That's not funny Cye, and believe me that's my choice." I said. We left the mall, as we approached the house, again I got dizzy. "Cye, something is wrong. I feel something inside of my stomach." "That's properly that sexual tension trying to escape." She said we both laughed. We parked the car and went to the front door and the door was a little open. We looked at each other. "Daddy", Cye yelled, "mama". We both kind of wished that we had our guns. But we traded them in for the good life. I slowly pushed the door open and eased inside. There was no sound, no one. "Mama", I yelled. Where are the party decorations? "We're getting played," Cye said. "They're just fooling around". "Alright Mama, and Daddy this ain't funny no more, where are you." Cye said. "Wc slowly walked up the stairs. Nothing was out of order. Cye walked into her parent's bedroom and fell to her knees. Screams and tears of "No, no, mama, daddy" I pushed the door behind her to see the image of her mother lying in a pool of blood on the bed, hands tied to the bed and one foot tied to the post. She was naked with blood running down between her legs. Her father was tied in a chair, his mouth was duck taped and his eyes was duck taped at the eyebrow so that he had to look forward he couldn't shut them. He had to witness the violation of his wife. He sat there dead bleeding from the gunshot wound in the middle of his forehead. His eyes were focus on his wife. Even though he was dead you could still see tears in his eyes. Everything was moving so slow. What seemed like minutes were just seconds. "My baby I screamed, where is my baby. I ran from room to room looking for my child. I was hysterical. I didn't want to believe what was happening. "Carletha, where are you? Mama, mama where are you" My heart raced faster and faster as I approached the room I stayed in. I saw blood trailing from under the door. Bullet holes were in the door. Fear entered my heart. I didn't want to open the door not wanting to see what was on the other side. I was moving in slow motion. I opened the door and screamed until there was nothing left. My mama was sitting in a pool of blood with a gun in her hands and a bullet hole in her head. Her lifeless body was up against the opened bathroom door. I was frozen I couldn't move. Time must have stood still for a couple of seconds. I couldn't stop yelling and screaming, then I remembered, my baby. "Where is my baby? Carletha, Carletha." I saw the blood trailing from the bathroom. The blood rushed to my brain, I rushed into the bathroom and saw my baby in the tub, cold and blue. For the first time in my life I lost control. The next thing I remembered was a lot of men with guns holding me, trying to pry me away from my baby. I was in the tub, holding her, she had duck tape on her mouth and around her legs and arms. I thought she was dead she was not moving. I held her and rocked her as if she was an infant. I thought there was nothing I could have done to deserve this. But in my mind I knew, "you reap what you sow". I had nightmares for the next six months, as I bounced from one mental institution to the next. After two years they decided that I wasn't a treat to myself or to anyone else in society. So they let me leave. They had told me my child was alive and the strength to get well came from wanting to see her again. I had heard Cye was also in an institution. She had gotten released and later turned to drugs and alcohol. After my release I didn't have anywhere to go. My money was gone and I was in California where I didn't know anyone. I went back to the house where we use to live. It was now a parking lot, a condominium for seniors. I walked around the parking lot to the beach side trying to get the thoughts of the past out of my head. I looked at what I thought was a cardboard tent hidden close to the marina. It was boxes tied up with string and sheets and I it Looked like someone lived there. As I passed I noticed a body and I could see their hands covering their face so the sun wouldn't come through. I stopped in my tracks when I noticed aunt Keysha's wedding band on her dirty hand. I was upset. My instincts told me to grab the brick lying on the fence and beat the shit out of them until they told me where they got the ring from. I grabbed the brick, but the person moved. They sat up, it was a woman. I couldn't believe my eyes. I moved in closer to get a better look. It was Cye. "Cye" I yelled. The girl looked up at me with a blank look. She was dirty and smelled like she been drinking for weeks. "Who the fuck are you?" she said. "It's me Cye, Tee, Teeka, you know who I am?" "You ain't Tee, she's dead, they all dead." She said lowering her head as if was talking to the ground. "Mama and daddy are dead, Tee, aunt Lolo and Carletha are dead. I don't know why I'm not dead." "Cye, it's me I'm not dead and Carletha is not dead. Cye, I need you to help me find her." I told her. "She's dead, mama's dead, daddy's dead, aunt Lolo is dead." Cye became hysterical and started crying and I started crying also. I tried to calm her down. "Cye you remember how we use to run the North End. How we were on top, had everything we wanted. Cye remember when I shot you because I thought you were fucking my man Jason? Come on Cye I know you remember." I sat down in her tent and we hugged each other so tight. She wouldn't let me go. She looked up at me with tears running down her face leaving a trail of dirt looking like a train track on her dirty face. "They're dead Tee, everybody's dead." Cye said. "We are not Cye, we have to pull our family back together. I don't like seeing you like this we have to get you help." I said. "Cye I can't help you unless you want to get help. You have to want to help yourself, are you ready." She bowed her head. "I don't like what I've become I need help Teeka, I had no one to turn to except the streets. My sister blames me for my parents murder and she hasn't talked to me." The streets are eating me alive I never thought I would end up like this." "Cye we've always helped each other and had each other's back. That hasn't changed. We have to fight to get our life back." I said as I helped her up and out from her cardboard tent. I hugged her and told her I loved her. The smell of her body was nauseating. The dirt caked up on her yellow skin made her look two shades darker, her clothes were dirty and the jeans she wore had brown stains on them as though she shitted on herself. Her jeans had dirt spots at the knees. I assume she had to suck and fuck to survive. Tears rolled down my face as I remembered how beautiful she once was and how I looked up to her. She hugged me tighter and said, "Teeka, please help me. I feel so lost and alone." "You are not alone I'm here. I will help you, Cyerisa Collins. But you must be committed to get straight." I said. We held each other, both crying both deep in thought. I didn't mind the nauseating smell and her foul breath. Then she asked "Teeka is Carletha alive?" "Yes, your sister keeps in contact with her. You got to get well so you can help me get her back." I pulled back from her and said, "Now you need some hot water." She looked at me and managed a faint smile. I thought I saw the old Cye somewhere in those eyes.

12

Mama Raised A Killer II

Chapter 2   Getting our Life's back

I found a job at a temp service and Cye went to a 90 day inpatient treatment center. I think she needed more counseling from the murders then treatment. I found out that my daughter was with judge Collins Cye's sister. Although I wanted to go get her, I had nowhere to raise her. Cye and I planned to stay in California while we tried to pull our life's back together. We both knew in our heart we had to find the killers of our family. While Cye was in treatment I spent my nights at the library looking up old newspapers. I found out that one of the suspects was shot by mama and later caught. It seems it was a mob hit so the papers say. The suspects name was Mark Gucci. They couldn't find any mob ties to uncle DC or aunt Keysha so they convicted Mark Gucci and closed the case. I was speechless their family is still looking for me, out here in

13

California? My mind raced back to the time I first met the Gucci brothers John and George. They were trying to make Cye and I sell their drugs. We later started buying from them until they couldn't handle the quantity of drugs we needed to supply the mid west. They had to turn us on to their connection for a fifty thousand dollar price tag. We built our empire and it grew to making a hundred thousand a week. The Gucci brothers tried to take over our business. I remember when they shot my mother while having some of their workers stick up the pool hall, our place of business. I remember when I caught George Gucci at his doctor's office. I can still see the look in his eyes when I put the cold steel gun to his head and asked him did he know who I was. I can still hear the thump of his body hitting the ground when he jumped out the window fearing for his life. Tears begin to form in my eyes when I remember holding Carl's body that was bullet ridden compliments of John Gucci. The image of John's body lying next to Carl just didn't seem right. I didn't think it was fair for him to take the only man that I ever loved. Giving his life wasn't enough even though I had put three bullets in his head. Now even in death the Gucci brothers have again taken the people I love. My anger turned to rage. Revenge will guide my life until I settle the score or die trying. I didn't go to work the next day. I had to think, is the Gucci family still looking for me? I had to be careful. I can't get my daughter with this hanging over me. I have to find the killers before they find me. I have to tell Cye. If she's down with me fine, if not I still have to have closure. I talked to my daughter once a week. I didn't want her to forget about me. I told her I would be coming to get her soon. I told Judge Collins that her sister was doing fine and we will be together when I pick up Carletha. She told me something I didn't expect. My mother had a $100,000. Insurance policy and the company had been looking for me to pay me off. All I needed was a death certificate. I had a lot of unfinished business and the money would help us. I went down to the city clerk and got mama's death certificate and got the check from the insurance company and deposited it. I went to see Cye and told her what was going on. I felt she would have time to think about what she wanted to do. She had two more weeks before she would be released. I found us an apartment. I bought a few things not much furniture in case we had to leave in a hurry. The next two weeks I did a lot of research. I spent days at the library on the internet trying to trace the Gucci family. In the evening I dressed down and started buying drugs in Compton. After a few days I had a steady runner who would cop for me. I gained his trust and he started telling me about who runs the drugs in Compton. It was the Gucci family through cousins and uncle's. I checked my list and found the names of three of the Gucci relatives the dope fiend told me about. Now I had a place to start. Dave my runner liked me he thought I was a user. I led him to believe no different. I started letting him get high when I bought drugs. I told him that I only got high with my man, who works and wants his drugs when he gets home. I couldn't believe he went for that one. It was four days before Cye got out and I had Dave buy some drugs for me. Only this time he took me with him because he wanted to get high right away, he was sick, his body needed some drugs to function normal. We went to a nice house a few blocks away. When the door was opened I was surprise to see a young white boy and two black men. The focus was on me even though I was dressed down. "Who is this Dave," the white man asked. "This is a friend of mine Key, I mean Keysha" Dave said. Keysha was my alias that I always used when I didn't want to use my name. I got it from my aunt. "Hey, Key I'm Dom" the white man said. I didn't say a word I just nodded because I didn't know if it was a set up. After the transaction we started to leave and Dom said. "Why don't you stay and get off here Dave?" "Can I?" Dave replied while sniffling and wiping his nose with his arm sleeve. "You can go in the basement take her with you." I spoke up. "I don't get high. I just cop for my old man. Dave

17

wanted to hook me up to a good connect so I brought him here to cop." "You don't get high?" one of the black guys said as he raised his gun and cocked it. Everybody froze, all eyes were on Dom. His decision would end my life. I thought it was over and I should have known better not to be strapped going to a drug house. "Hold up Mike," Dom said. "Come have a drink with me, you do drink don't you?" I was really scared I had flashbacks of me being raped be Carl's old crew. With my sexiest tone I said, "sure, I drink socially, I'll have a glass of wine." Dom was trying to hit on me. He really was nice and we talked about thirty minutes. Dave returned from the basement he was ready and walked to the door. I got up from the bar and walked over to Dom extended my hand and smiled. "Thanks for the drink, Don" "My name is Dom short for Dominique, Dom Gucci not Don." He took offense for me calling him Don, I have to remember that. "Can I see you again take you to lunch some time." He asked. I knew I had his number at that moment, but I'm not into white boys. "I got a

Mama Raised A Killer II

man, but thanks anyway" Then we walked out the door and I tried to shake all my curves through the big clothes I had on, walking behind Dave. I felt the eyes of Dom and his boys looking at my body. After I left Dave I went back to the apartment. The turn of events where now in my favor. I could use this way to get knowledge of the organization. When Cye comes out I could introduce her to Dom.

19

Chapter 3 The Set up

For the next two weeks I put my plan in motion. I was unaware which way Cye would go but either way she is still the sister that I never had. I bought two cars and a blue Toyota Camry an old model black cutlass with tinted windows. I didn't drive the Cutlass at all I just keep it in the garage. Cye was waiting for me at the door the day she was released. I must admit she looked real good. Her color was back, her smile was beautiful and you could tell she was getting her confidence back. I took her to the apartment and we stayed up all night talking. We talked about the past and the future. We went over our mistakes we made in the past and talked about our future plans. I showed her the drugs I bought and told her about Dom Gucci. Cye wanted revenge of her parents. She understood the consequences. We both were willing to do whatever we had to do, including dying if it came to that. We again made a pact to always no matter what watch each other's back. The next morning we went shopping and I bought Cye a car. She wanted a red convertible Chrysler Sebring. She looked like a model in that car and the salesman wanted to take her out. "Something's never change" I said. "I guess you still got it." "I never lost it Tee I just smothered it for a while, now I'm back." She said. We went back to the mall Cye needed a red outfit with matching coat. After going from store to store buying whatever Cye wanted I heard someone calling, "Key" as we walked down the corridor. Hey Keysha, Cye and I keep talking and walking. Then this big black man grabs my arm. "Hey Keysha, Dom wants to holla at you." I forgot my alias for a minute and Cye was looking at me strange but she went with the flow. "Who," I said. The white man appeared in front of me. "Oh you don't remember having a drink with me," I thought it was cool that he didn't say where I met him. He got a point for that. "Hi Dom" I said. "I'm a little hurt" he said. "Why, cause I didn't go to lunch with you?" I asked. "Naw, because I didn't know you was this beautiful, and you wouldn't let me see you again." He said. "This must be your sister, you girls look alike. Can I buy you girl's lunch?" "No thanks, this is my sister Cece." He looked at Cye and spoke then looked back at me. "I would still like to take you to lunch or a movie, can I get your cell number to call you" he said. "Dom, Thanks but I told you I got a man." I said. "That's cool, here is my number just in case, or you can use it and you don't need Dave, nice meeting you Cece, Let's bounce" he said as he walked off with his boys. "Cye was speechless, "you got it going on with a fine white boy and you play him" she said. "Girl he was all over you" "Cye that's Dom, Dom Gucci I told you about him. Shit I was trying to hook you up with him. Now we got to go to plan B." "So I guess I'm supposed to get use to answering to Cece?" she asked. "That's your new name sis." We both laughed and then we shopped until we dropped.

Mama Raised A Killer II

Chapter 4

Gaining Trust From an Enemy

Cye coming home made me happy. We sat up and talked like we use too years ago. We decided that we both needed to find the killers of our parents. I met Dave and gave him some of the drugs I have been buying. In turn I needed to know where I could buy some guns. He told me his cousin had a hook up. I met his cousin and bought me a small arsenal. Four handguns two nine millimeters and two glocks and three AK automatic, drug dealers weapons and a lot of extra ammunition.. Later on that morning I agreed to meet Dom at a restaurant in LA. But I told him I will not go out with him with an entourage. We had a nice lunch and I told him I had to get home. He enticed me to have a drink with him at his house. "One little drink then you can leave." He said. "I'm really enjoying your company Key," "I'm having a good time to, but I got to get home" I said "just one drink." I couldn't resist getting to gain his trust so I agreed. As we pulled up to the house his two body guards came running out as though they knew he was pulling up. By the time we parked they were coming down the sidewalk and opened the door. Out the corner of my eye I saw a black car pulling out of the parking place across the street. Dom got out the car and held the door open for me. His guys had a question look on their face. "He's never did that before," Mike said. "he must think you are special" I walked ahead of everybody, and said "I am special." Both the guys were standing there looking at me when Dom said, "You guys never seen a pretty black woman before?" Not with you" Mike said. All three guys started laughing. Just then the car appeared with the window down and shots firing. The men didn't have time to react. They were caught laughing. Mike and his partner were hit first almost dead center in the heart. Without thinking I sprung into action and knocked Dom down while pulling out my nine millimeter from my purse. I got off three shots before I was hit in the arm and went down. The car speed off and Dom got up on his knees still looking around like some little punk. He looked at me and said "are you alright?" "I'm hit Dom," I said felling the blood run down my arm. "Come on we got to get you inside." As soon as we got inside the police were pulling up. Dom told me to go upstairs and he will be back. The bullet only grazed me and the blood was all on my clothes. I went upstairs and peered out the window blinds to see what was going on. I saw the police officer's talk to Dom, for what seem like hours. I got some towels and soaked the blood off me and looked at my wound. It was superficial I won't need to go to the doctors. When I got back to the window I saw the coroner put sheets over the two guys lying dead in the street. I saw them put Dom in the car as he looked up to the window. His eyes told me to stay put. When they finally left after four hours I went downstairs and double locked all the doors and windows. The police were still outside doing their investigation so I laid down on the bed upstairs and feel asleep. I woke up feeling wet lips on my face. "What the fuck are you doing" "I'm sorry, I just wanted to tell you thanks, you saved my life. You took a bullet for me. I will never forget that." He said. "you don't have to be kissing all over me for that, you can just say thanks" I said still trying to play hard to get. Yea, I took a bullet for him, and he is going to pay for it, with his life. "Do you need to go to the doctor?" he asked. I showed him the wound. "It's not that bad, I'll be alright, I need to get home. Can you take me back to my car, please" "Whatever you want, Key anything you ever need you call me. I mean it" he looked so sincere. "Please take me back to my car. I need to take care of this wound." I said. "You know, Key both of my boys got killed and I could use someone close to me that's not scared to do work. You think you might be down with that?" he asked. "I don't know I watched my ex's back until he died. I'm not trying to get caught up out here in Cali. Besides most men don't trust women to have their back" "You saved my life, I could be dead now if you weren't around. I'd rather have you close to me, you got a lot of heart. Just think about it. I'll pay you three thousand a week." He said. I begin to think this is too good to be true, I couldn't have planned this better myself. I'll see how far he's willing to go and how bad he wants me. "That's all cool, but I can't watch your back if no one is watching my back." I said. 'You can hire whoever you want, I'll pay them two thousand a week." He said. "wait a minute, suppose I bring a woman, that means you will be around two women all the time watching your back." "I trust you, Key, I'd rather have someone I can trust then someone I must always watch, thinking they might set me up." "How you going to invite me out on a date and have me watch your back. What do you want from me, Dom?" All I want is for you to watch my back, be there if I need you. As far as us kicking it, if it happens it happens. I'm not going to pressure you. I like being around you" "I have to think about it, give me a couple of days, okay" I asked. "Come on let me take you back,

27

before I get sentimental. We left his house and I could see how uncomfortable he was. He kept looking over his shoulders. He kept one hand on his gun in his waist band. I kind of felt sorry for him, someone had killed his top boys and he was worried. "You okay," I asked "yea, I'm ok" he said. We didn't talk much on the ride to my car. Before I got out I said, "Dom, call me tomorrow, we can work something out. But I'm going to tell you up front, my sister and I cannot be controlled. If you want some puppets you better get someone else. If we suppose to have your back you have to listen to us, sometimes anyway." "I hear you Key, I guess it's just getting to me, I almost died today. I have to be more careful." He said. "Here is my number I got to go if you need to talk to me I'm a phone call away." "Thanks, Key," he said. I went straight for my car and didn't look back. I felt his eyes on me all the way. When I got it my car I saw him pulling off like someone chasing him. I thought to myself he is out of his league.

Mama Raised A Killer II

When I got to the house Cye was resting on the couch, "I see you made it home in one piece." Cye said sarcastically. "That is not funny Cye, and by the way I hope you know we are even." I said. "Even you shot me because you thought I was fucking your man, I shot you for business." I thought Cye had gotten serious on me and I was too tired to defend myself. "So we not even?" I asked. "Girl I'm just messing with you, let me look at that wound. Teeka, we sisters, in blood and death nothing or no one will ever come between us again" Cye said while looking me straight in my eyes. "You're right Cye, nothing or no one, I love you girl" I said. "Girl you are a hard cold killer, what does love have to do with it." She said. We both laughed. Cye bandaged up my wound and gave me some pain pills. I laid down and feel asleep. The next morning I was awakened by my cell phone. It was Dom. "Good morning Key, how you doing? You ready to go to work." "What, it's only nine o'clock, what kind of business you got this early?" I asked rubbing the sleep out of my eyes. "I got an appointment at 11:30, you coming or not. I usually go by myself, I'll be alright." "No wait we will be there. Where you want us to meet you?" "I want you to come by yourself" he said. "No I come with my partner or I don't come at all. She watches my back while I watch yours, we made a deal." "It's hard for me to trust you so soon, how you think I'm going to trust someone else too." "I trusted you enough to save your life, now you got to trust me. Where you want to meet me?" I asked. "Ok, meet me where we had lunch in LA, then you guys follow me and don't get lost. One hour, bye" he hung up. I jumped up because I didn't tell Cye about our job offer. Cye was already dressed. She looked as good as see did when we were young. "Where you going this early" I asked. "Nowhere, it has been so long since I've felt this good about myself. I'm just trying to get back to my fine looking self." "All that's cool girl, but do you want to go to work with me, making 2k a week for starters" I asked. "Who we going to work for getting that much bread?" she asked. "Dom, Dom Gucci. What?" How we going to work for someone who's family killed our parents?" "If we work for him it will be easier to find the whole family and the persons responsible for our parent's death." I responded. "I have to get dress we have to meet him in an hour. Make sure you bring the girls" Within an hour we were pulling up in front of the restaurant. I noticed Dom's car at the entrance of the restaurant. I decided to wait and follow him as he requested. After about twenty minutes he came out along with a young black female. " Look at this, white boy thinks he's a Mack daddy" I said. "Well as long as he's paying me 2K a week he can Mack to his death" Cye said. Dom looked around to see my car he smiled and got in the car with the female. When they pulled off two men came running out the restaurant and jumped in a car and sped off behind them. They almost hit our car pulling away from the curb. Cye and I looked at each other and followed them a distance

31

away. We stayed close enough so we could see the car with Dom and the female in it and we could still see the car with the two men. After about fifteen minutes the car pulled on a tree lined street. Nice cars in every drive way. All the lawns where cut and maintained with their bushes trimmed to match the landscaping of each house. Dom and the female pulled up to a circle driveway house and got out. The men following stopped at the house next door and parked. Cye and I drove passed them, pulled up the street and parked. We could see the house and the car with the men in it through our rear view mirror. Dom and the female got out of the car and the female used a key to open the door. " She must live there" I said. Cye and I watched the situation for ten minutes. Then to two men got out their car and went up to the door. Before reaching the porch the men pulled out guns and cocked them. They burst through the door that must have been left open. "It's on now, what we goin do Tee" Cye asked. "This doesn't look good, something is going down" I said. Cye reached in her purse and pulled out two nine millimeters pearl handle automatic guns for me and 2 glocks' for herself. "Let's do this, I miss the excitement and the rush we use to get when we taken care of business." Cye said. "you were the one who wanted out the business, then convinced me to get out." I said as we exited the car. "Yea, I know, but look what it got us, everybody is dead any way." She said." "Look Cye, stay focus and watch my back, are you cool" I said. "I'm alright Tee, let's do this." She said "Just follow my lead, we don't know what's up in there but make sure you have my back and I'll have yours." I put my guns up and walked to the door and knocked. I could hear some yelling and I could see the men with their guns out. The knock startled the people inside. It took a couple of minutes before the female came to the door. She was a nice looking dark girl. Her makeup was flawless. Her hair was cut short and she had on designer clothes. "I'm sorry to bother you but me and my sister's car ran out of gas and my cell phone is dead. Can I please use the phone it will only take a *minute to call me husband." I said. She paused for a minute then she said hold on. When she went to get the phone Cye and I came in and stood. We could see the men with the guns standing over Dom. They had their eyes on us and not on Dom. They had their hands behind their backs but their dirty minds was on me and Cye. When the young lady came back with the phone, she reached out to give it to me. Before she had a chance to put it in my hand, Cye had her gun to the girl's temple. "Don't fucking move" Cye said. Before she could turn to look at Cye my gun was pointed at her chest. The guys pulled their guns out and pointed them at us. "If you don't drop your guns this bitch is dead" I said. Cye cocked her gun then pulled her other gun and pointed toward the men. "You better tell them to drop their guns or I'll pull this trigger right now," Cye said as she hit the girl in the mouth with the other gun still keeping her gun at her temple. The girl yelled in pain and said "drop your guns fools." The two men laid their guns down. "What's this about the girl managed to say* through the blood stained teeth in her mouth. "Who sent you here I don't have any product here. I didn't say a word I walked over to where Dom was sitting with his hands tied up. "You alright boss" I said. The room was quiet. Cye pushed the young lady in the room with the other guys. "They work for you" Dom tried to smile through bloody teeth and didn't say a word. I untied him and he picked up the guns that the two men had. "You want me to kill her, boss" Cye said. The girl started pleading for her life. "Please Dom, I'm sorry, don't do this Dom, think of your son" "Tonya did you think of your baby daddy when you set me up." Dom said. "That is the only reason you are still breathing, I don't want my son to be motherless. But, next time I catch you in my business I'll raise my son by myself." Cye and I kept our guns on the two men who looked confused. "She didn't tell you guys she had a son by me" Dom Asked. "No I didn't know, but it wouldn't matter to me, I'm in it for the money." One of the guys trying to be hard said. There are always those who believe that women are soft. I walked over to the man who was at least six foot three and I stood there in all my five feet five inches. Looked up in his eyes then shot him in his knee cap. "You'll be walking with a limp for the rest of your life. Now if you want me to solve that problem say something else." The men quenched in pain. The other man looked horrified. "These bitches are your back up which one you fucking" the woman screamed. "That ain't any of your business, you need to worry about getting out of here alive, then who getting fucked." I said. Dom looked at me for an answer, he walked up to me and asked "what you wanna do?" "If we kill one of them we got to kill them all, I'll do whatever you want." I said. "You handle it," he said. I whispered to him, "Dom, you have to get a reputation and respect to be in this game." "Just handle it any way you want." He shouted. Everybody could hear our conversation. Now they were uncertain as to what might happen to them. I looked at Cye and she must have read my mind. You see, Cye's mother was raped while her father was killed watching. I was violated by some disgruntled workers. I guess somehow we wanted some sort of revenge to make us feel better. She again hit the woman with the gun on top of her head. She yelled out in pain. "Take your clothes off, Cye said. Everybody take your clothes off, all of them. Before the woman could complain Cye hit her again. Blood was running down her forehead as she quickly started taking her clothes off. "I'll be in the car, give me your keys" I tossed my keys to Dom and he left the house. Fear begin to set in for the three people in the room. Two were bleeding and the other one standing mute but naked. Dam he had a large tool. "Since you worried about who Dom is fucking, I wanna know who you fucking. Are you fucking either one of these guys?" I asked. The woman just shook her head no. "What you think, girl" I asked Cye. "You think she fucking one of these guys?" "I would fuck the one with the big dick, that's the one" We both turned to look at the guy. "you, I want you to fuck this bitch, right here right now," Cye pushed the girl on the floor. She was screaming no, don't rape me. "Girl he ain't raping you, he keeping you from dying" The girl laid on the floor and open her legs. "Put your legs behind your head, lift them up" Cye said. I went over to the guy and pushed him towards the floor. The other guy was staring and holding his bloody leg. "You don't move" I pointed to the wounded guy. The other guy started to get an erection looking at the fine piece of ass in front of him. He knew he always wanted some, now he was getting his opportunity. When he got on top of the girl she started screaming. "That's too big, I can't take that" Cye bent down and put the barrel of the gun in her mouth. "Suck on this and be quiet." The guy's dick wouldn't go in, it was too big. I walked behind him and hit him with the butt of my gun "force it in." He pushed as hard as he could and the girl screamed in pain as her insides were ripped wide open, the gun barrel Cye had in her mouth made her gag. Tears formed in her eyes and the cries turned to joy as the pain started to stop. The guy was pumping harder and harder. She *begins to fight the pain and enjoy the moment. She was meeting him stroke for stroke. Cye still had the gun in the girl's mouth. She was licking it like a Popsicle. I think Cye was getting turned on herself. She was sweating and her eyes were getting bigger the more she watched. This was supposed to be torture but everybody seems to be enjoying it except me and the man with the bullet in his head. "Alright that's enough." I walked up to the man and women lying on top on each other. "If you guys ever see Dom, you need to cross the street cause if our paths cross again it will be a different ending. Come on girl" I grabbed Cye by the arm and we backed out of the house. When we got back to the car Dom was sitting on the hood smoking a cigarette. "What was that about?" I asked. "That was my son's mama trying to set me up. This is the second time she has done that." He said. "You let her get away with it" I said. "Look, I'm not trying to tell you what to do, but if you going to make money in this business, you have to be ruthless, you have to have a reputation."*

"That's why I need people I can trust, I told you that. With me being white selling drugs in a black neighborhood it gets me tried a lot. Again you saved my life, Key. You girls are down I need you around me 24/7." He said. We all got in the car and took Dom back to the restaurant to pick up his car. On the ride to his car Dom said, "Ladies I have a proposition for you, if you are interested." "What kind of proposition, we don't do threesomes" Cye said. "Naw, I want you ladies to go in business with me." "I don't know if we want to sell drugs, Dom." I said. "Not selling, distributing and collecting. You think about it and we'll talk tomorrow" He threw us a pack of money wrapped in a rubber band as he got out of the car and got in his own. "Nine o'clock tomorrow in Compton" he said as he pulled off not waiting for an answer. Cye and I looked at each other. "Do you think this town is ready for us? She asked. "Cye we have to remember what our mission is, and by the way, I seen your ass getting hot in the panties back at the house. But I couldn't figure out was you hot for the guy with the big dick, or the girl who was sucking you off." "Fuck you Tee, she was sucking the gun not me" "Shit I couldn't tell." We both laughed. "It has been awhile without sex for both of us" I said. We made it home and counted the money. Five thousand dollars we took a thousand each and a put three thousand up for a rainy day. We talked and plotted until the early morning hours. Our lives were beginning to change.

Chapter 5   Getting Back In The Game

It was a week before we heard from Dom. He called me at 11:00AM on a Sunday and asked me if I could meet him. I told him I would not be alone. So Cye and I packed our arsenal and went to meet up with Dom. We met in a park and was informed that he was going to pick up a shipment of product. I got in Dom's car and we drove about a mile away. Cye was following a distance in our car. When we stopped I told him I would act like his lady. Cye stayed a block away in the background in case we were being set up. After fifteen minutes a car pulled up and two Mexican's got out. "What's up meda," one of them said. "Everything's cool" Dom said while handing them some dap. "Who's the pretty girl, and why you with her, here?" The second Mexican said while he put his hand on his gun in his waste. I put my hand in my purse, as Dom said. "Hold up my man this my woman" as he reaches over and stuck his hot tongue in my mouth. I must admit he caught my off guard and it felt good. "This is Shante" he said. "Ain't she fine?" The Mexican looked at my reaction, and then looked at him. Dom begin smiling and said. "Let's get down to business." The Mexican said "Follow me." He led the way to the back room in a vacant warehouse and his partner followed us. I tried to sneak a look back to see if I could see Cye. When we entered the room two more guys were standing around holding automatic weapons. "Dom threw his suitcase on the table and said, "Here is the money" One of the Mexicans reached for the suitcase my gun met his temple before his hand reached the handle. "Hold on partner, we need to see the merchandise first" I said. I could hear each weapon being cocked. The tension was building. "Hold on" Dom said, "Your lady comes in here and disrespect us by pulling a gun on my man" the Mexican said. "You not going to get the bread until we see you got our merchandise. That's only business" I said. "You bitch" one of the Mexican said as they pointed their guns at me. I'm not going to be too many bitches" I said. "Hold on Jose" Dom managed to say. "I ought to blow you and this bitch away" he said while looking straight at me. My hand was steady and my gun was ready. "I won't be going by myself, we all be leaving here together." I said. Jose motioned for one of his boys with the automatic, but they didn't move. It was then he noticed the laser red light on his chest then Jose looked down to see a red light on his chest. Everybody looked around to find where the laser lights where coming from. "Can we just complete our business so we all can go home to our families?" I yelled and I put my weapon down to my side. "Come on Jose, this is my protection, let's do our business and go. Jose was mad but he was no fool. He didn't know how many guns were outside. He told his man to get the package. He returned with two suitcases full of drugs. It had to be 50 kilos of cocaine. "Everybody relax" Dom said. "Here is your money let me test the drugs and we are out of here." All the Mexican's were looking at Jose I don't think they really had the heart to die if it came to that. Jose waved his hand and Dom tested the drugs looked at me and said everything is cool. I pushed the suitcase to the man I had held the gun on keeping my eyes on his every move. Jose's men still watched the laser jumping on their chest. "No disrespect gentlemen, I have to protect my man's interest. Can we leave now?" I said. "Dom you know we won't be doing business again" Jose said. "You right Jose, next time I'll deal with your boss, not you." Dom turned around to leave and I eyed the other man and backed out the room following him. The laser light was still on the men as I left the room. As soon as the laser faded away Jose yelled in Spanish to get my drugs back. We had just got inside our car when the gun shots start pouring out. "Come on Dom, pull off." Jose's gun shots shattered the back window as we were speeding off. After a block I said "Turn round Dom." "What? Why we need to turn around?" "We left Cye back there."I yelled. "I'm not turning around" he said. I pulled my gun out and shot at his ear blood starting flowing from the light scar on his ear. You shot me you black bitch. "You better turn this mother fucking car around now or I'll be the last bitch you see." Dom hit the brakes and turned the car around to the surprise of the guys shooting at us. I begin shooting out the window when the men started to fall. Cye was hiding in a corner until she saw us turn around, now she was blasting away. Before the car got back down the block, two of the men were dead. I took out Jose and the last guy standing before the car came to a stop. After a few minutes Cye came running to the car. "Get in" I said. "Look Key, all the four men are dead, I'm going to see if anyone else is inside. I don't want to be looking over my shoulders because we left someone alive." Dom was shaking like a leaf. Cye didn't even wait for an answer she just ran into the warehouse. I jumped out and followed her with both of my guns drawn. The scared ass Dom burned rubber getting off the block. "I should've killed that ass hole," I said. "In due time Teeka, in due time."Cye said with a devilish look on her face. "What's going on Cye, you know we got everybody." She dashed in the warehouse with me close on her heels guns ace deuce like we were the police. We crepe in slowly in case someone was hiding. I was on one side of the room and Cye was on the other. Cye took off running to the table, then it hit me they left the money. The smile on her face spoke for itself when I reached the table and saw all the money in the suitcase. We looked at each other and smiled then the gangster in us took over again as we ran out the warehouse with the suitcase and guns drawn ready to kill. I walked back to the car looking over our shoulders. The car she was driving was hidden two blocks away. We jump in and sped off. Our adrenaline was in high gear, it was like we were high or something. My heart was beating so hard I looked at Cye, "Girl we getting too old for this shit" "Not when the rewards are this good" she said while holding the suitcase in her hand. "Teeka, I knew you would come back for me" "I will always have your back Cyrisa" We both laughed and didn't speak again until we reached the house to put the car up.

Mama Raised A Killer II

Chapter 6

Money Falling in Our Hands

We counted the money at the house which took us over two hours. It was two hundred and fifty thousand dollars. Cye and I just sat there lost in our on individual thoughts. "This is a lot of money" she said looking at the large numbers of stacked bills on the table. "We have enough money to start over anywhere, Tee." "Yea, I know, is that what you want?" I asked. "Is that what you want, Tee?" We were both silent for a few minutes. We knew that whatever decision we made we both would have to honor it. "Well Teeka, we have always had money. We have had a million dollars before that we made.

We are always going to be able to make money. But this money won't bring my parents back." Tears formed in her eyes. "I know nothing is going to bring them back. But I would be able to have a little closer knowing that the people that were responsible for their deaths can join them in death." "I don't care about the money Cye, I want the people that did that to our parents dead. The cold blooded way they were killed torches me every night. I want their whole family to feel this pain. I want revenge." I didn't realize I was crying until Cye came over and hugged me. Our wet tears collided with each others, face to face as we hugged tighter and tighter. As we embraced we both knew that our life would never be the same. We both knew that we would die trying to revenge our family before we continue to live with this guilt and pain. With tears in my eyes and snot running down my nose I said. "Cye, if something should happen to me could you please promise me to take care of my daughter." "Tee, nothing is going to happen to you or me." "Cye, please just tell me you would" I begged. "Ok, I promise." She said."I'm going to take a long shower and when I get back we'll get our plan and priorities straight." She smiled and sat down and started to put the money up. When I got out the shower my cell phone was blowing up. Dom had the nerve to call me twenty four times. I didn't answer I'm going to let him wait a while. "The nerve of his punk ass calling me after he left us in the middle of his bull shit. I can't wait to settle up with him" I said. "Come on Tee, we got to keep thinking we have to stay one step ahead of them." Cye said, we have found his weakness, it's you. I can't tell you how to play this, but if you let him get next to you we could get his whole family. I don't want just him because as you can see he is too scared to hurt anybody so he could not have killed our parents. I don't even see why he is the game. His people set him up to be something that he is not." "I see where you coming from." "He doesn't have the heart that's why he needs us to survive. So don't let our on pride keep us from reaching our goal." Cye said. "You're right, I just want him to think for a minute. Let him hold on to that dope that he can't get off without us. He will call us with a sweeter deal. Do you think that he thinks we took the money?" I asked. "He didn't think about it when his ass left us. But I bet the boss of them Mexican's will be looking at him thinking he double crossed them." Cye said. "That's more of the reason to make him sweat, at least until tomorrow. I don't want him to think that we got the money and left town." "Tee, whatever you decide to do, either way I will down all the way, til death if it goes that way. I'm getting ready to shower and get some sleep I'll talk to you in the morning" Cye said as she headed up the stairs. My thoughts continued to the past. I thought about mama and how she was always by my side and always gave us the right advice. I thought about the only man I ever loved Carl. Tears begin to run down my face as I thought about my daughter. She doesn't have a father and she doesn't have her mother with her. I want to call off all this revenge stuff and go get my baby.

The thoughts of my uncle and aunt being brutally vandalized and my mother with the bullet hole in her head brought me back to reality. Rage built up inside me and before I knew it I was dialing Dom's number. "Hey Dom this is me" forgetting for a minute my alias. "Key how are you doing? Dam Key, you could have called and let me know if you were alright." "If you were so worried about how I was you wouldn't have left us." I snapped. "Key my thoughts were on all the product I had, I couldn't get caught up by the po po, you feel me." "I just know you left Cye and me in the middle of your mess." "I'm sorry Key." "I think they had a look out, we thought we saw a shadow." I said. "Oh naw, that is not good when could we meet we have to talk?" he asked. "Cye just went to bed and I'm not doing no business without her." "This is not business I want to see you and talk to you. You almost blew my head off at least you can see if I'm ok" he said trying to make me feel guilty. "You aren't really cut out for this line of work, you should understand loyalty is with your people. You should have been loyal to us, we the ones got your back." "Ok, Key I'm sorry, put what I feel for you is not only business. I want you to get to know me better, meet my family and be the woman I know you are." He said. The key word that had my mind running was family. For me to get closer to his family I will do anything and I do mean anything. "Dom we said we would do business together I didn't promise you anything."I said. "Keysha I know what we talked about, but every time I see you and every time you prove how down you are for me only gets me more attached to you. I really care about you as a woman more than an associate." He said. I remember the kiss and how I felt it almost took me off my square. This white boy had some game. "Dom, what do you want from me?" "All I want is for you to have an open mind and give a brother a chance." He said. We both had to chuckle about the last part. "Please Key, meet me for a little while when you ready to come back I will let you go. It's only 11:30 I know you don't go to bed this early." I couldn't let him think he could control me with his game. "Dom, I'm a little worn out from the day. You can call me in the morning and we can spend time together tomorrow. I hope your ear is all right. Remember if I wanted to hurt you I wouldn't have grazed your ear. Call me in the morning Dom goodnight." I hung up the phone not waiting for an answer. I could almost see Dom looking at the phone wondering what to take from what I said. I know he would have a lot of questions when he saw me. I have questions for him also about his family. I will sleep tonight knowing I am getting closer to my goal.

Chapter 7 Showing My Assets

The phone rang at exactly 11:00 o'clock. Of course I didn't answer the first call. When he called back I picked up the phone. "Hello" "Hi Key, we on for this morning?" he said. "Yes Dom where you do want to meet me?" "I'm in downtown Los Angeles. You can meet me on Beverly Blvd across from the Soffitel Hotel. There is a nice little restaurant on the corner." "Ok, I know where that is I'll be there at 1:00 O'clock." "That's cool you'll know who I am, I'll be the one smiling so much with a patched up ear" he said. "That's funny, I'll see you later." "Bye, Keysha." He hung up and I started to get ready. I had a lot of clothes that I never wore out here in California because I never had any where to go. I go out a two piece pants suit with a low back and showing just enough cleavage in the front. I let my hair drop across my left eye that made me look like a model off the run way with my short hair cut. I put on some two inch pumps just in case I had to get away fast. I was ready at 12:45. I talked to Cye and told her to call me in two hours. If I wasn't ready to come home I would let her know by asking "How's the dog?" Letting her know I was alright. Cye also told me take my 380 revolver with me. So I put it in my Prada purse. I arrived at the restaurant at 1:15 just a little fashionably late. Dom was sitting in the back booth. I must admit he looked good. He had on a nice pair of expensive jeans with a dress shirt and a jacket. His cologne smell was inviting. I don't know if it was the lack of male attention or was I really beginning to feel him. Again I had to remind myself of the mission at hand and 'I don't do white boys.' "Hi Keysha you look great, these flowers are for you." "Thanks Dom, why do you call me Key some times. Then other times you call me Keysha." I asked while smelling the flowers. "Well Keysha when I call you Key we are usually working or doing work. When I call you Keysha, that is a form of respect I have for you as a woman. I separate the two because I have the ultimate respect for you and I want to get to know Keysha as the woman." I begin to blush. This guy was beginning to make me tingle inside. I notice the looks we were getting from other people in the restaurant. The black women were looking at me mean. The black men had a smirk on their face. The white women looked at Dom with discuss. The white men looked at Dom and smiled wishing they could be in his shoes. The waitress was very pleasant as though she knew the looks we were receiving. We ate our meal and left. He said he wanted to take me on Sunset Blvd. to see the Hollywood walk of fame. We walked and talked he grabbed my hand and I started to melt. I was really feeling good. We didn't even notice a couple of guys following us. We were sharing each other's company getting to know each other. We walked up to La Brea Avenue then back to Vine Street. I had never seen this side of the world. I enjoyed seeing how the different nationalities and people. We turned on Vine and walked down a block from the avenue. Dom said his car was parked there. We were still holding hands and he had me smiling from ear to ear. He really was a funny guy. A horn blew that startled both of us. We looked to the street where the sound came from. The next think I knew someone hit Dom it the head with a gun but pushing him forward. Dom released my hand and he was struck again. I felt a hand smack me in the face. I put my purse up shielding my face from another smack. The Mexican caught the purse with his hand and the force knocked me to the ground. The other guy got out the car and both man approached Dom. "Dom where is my money?" the Mexican said. "Where is my dope?" Dom said. "I'm not bull shitting with you Dom, I don't care who your family is I want my money or drugs." The second guy put his gun to Dom's head. I pulled my purse down and acted like I was crying while grabbing my 380 automatic. I unlocked the safety but I keep my hand on the gun while it was in my purse. The guys were not paying any attention to me like I wasn't there. "Tito" Dom said. "I lost $250,000. The other night and I still didn't get my stuff. Some brothers were waiting on us I barely made it out alive. Look they almost shot my ear off. Dom took the bandage off his ear to show the men. I kept my ground waiting to see how this will play out. I know I could get one guy but both guys had their guns out. "Somebody set us up. Did you talk to Jose?" Dom asked. "Jose is dead, all my guys are dead. You are the only one alive." Dom said "that sounds like an inside job. Your boy Jose was mad when I told him I'm only going to deal with you. You can kill me now if you want to, but I already told my uncles that I was set up so they put a contract on your organization. You and your people won't be able to make no money. I want my 250k or my product." "I ain't got your money" Tito said. "Let me kill him Tito" the other guy said. While Tito thought about his consequences the other Mexican cocked his gun and put it to Dom's temple. I aimed and shot him once in the head. My bullet caught him behind his right ear and he fell to the ground. Tito turned around at me and attempted to shoot. He didn't have time he had dropped his gun to his side while he was thinking. He didn't react in time. Dom pulled a small gun from under his jacket and shot two times. Tito fell to the ground and clutched his stomach. Dom kicked him and said "You better get me my money." I was looking at the action when my phone rung my instincts took over. "Come on Dom, we have to get out of here." It was like Dom was in a trance but he looked at me and reacted. We walked slowly up the street as the crowd began to surround the fallen Mexicans. By the time we got to Dom's car we heard the police sirens. Dom started the car and we drove off like we weren't in a hurry. My cell phone rang again. "Hi Cye, yes I'm fine. How's the dog? I'll feed him when I get back home. I'll call you when I'm on my way." I hung up. My message in girl talk was. I'm ok I have something to tell you when I get home. Don't wait up for me. Dom drove up on the hill and we looked at the stars homes. We saw

Halle Barry's, Bruce Willis and Leonardo Dicapra's home sitting off what looked like a cliff. It was so beautiful. We rode down to Wilshire Blvd. "Dom, you know I underestimated you. I didn't think you had the heart to be in this game." I said. "Thanks, but Keysha I was trying to protect you. I don't want anything to happen to you." My heart sunk, I haven't heard that since Carl told me that. I was silent. Dom asked "What's wrong? Did I say something wrong?" "No I was just thinking about my past, my last man said he would protect me then he left me." "I'm sorry Keysha, I got something that's going to cheer you up." I didn't tell him that he died trying to protect me because his uncle killed my man. We pulled up on a side street and got out. We walked up Wilshire Blvd. and the stores looked like a magazine picture. Although the streets were full of people none where going in the stores. I didn't want to feel stupid but I had to ask. "I know the prices in these stores must be high, why isn't anyone going in the stores?" Dom looked at me with a puzzled look. "They don't let you in the stores unless you have an appointment or unless you are Paris Hilton." He smiled, I hadn't really notice how handsome he really was. His smile was perfect he had a dimple on his left side. If you saw him on the street dressed up you would think he was a model or entertainer. "Come on" he said as he pulled me into this boutique. When we got inside the lady said "Mr. Gucci how are you, and how is the family?" "Hi Crystal everybody is fine. This is my friend Keysha, she wants to try on some dresses." "Hi Keysha follow me, Dom you can set in the parlor and I'll have her model them for you. There is some coffee and donuts in there help yourself." the saleslady said. She pulled me in the backroom and showed me fifteen dresses and gowns none of them under a thousand dollars. I tried the first one on and she pointed me to a section that had mirrors and Dom was sitting there smiling. "You like that one?" he asked. "I don't know they are expensive." "Keysha I didn't ask you the price, do you like it? "Yes it's ok, but let me try on the rest" "Ok, but you choose any of them you like" "Dom I can't let you buy these for me" "Keysha just try the dresses on, let me decide what I can do" Dom has another side that I had never seen before today. I think I like it. I tried on all the dresses and could not decide on which one out of the four I liked the most. The sales lady was very attentive. I wasn't use to that I was the only one in the store. Dom got up and said he'll be right back he went over to the sales lady. I didn't see any money or credit cards exchange. He then said let's go. I knew I couldn't afford the dresses but what woman doesn't like shopping? I told myself I will be coming back to buy the dresses before I leave California. Dom held the door open for me as we were leaving the store. He watched my demeanor. My look was disappointed. When I stepped out he said "Keysha you forgetting your dresses." I turn around and the sales lady was rushing to the door with four bags. A big smile assumed my face. I told Dom thanks and reached out for his hand. He grabbed my hand and put his arm around my shoulders. We walked back to the car like we were so in love. But I cannot forget the mission. I cannot lose focus. We drove back down Beverly Blvd. and the police were everywhere. "Dam, Key where you park?" Dom asked. "I parked in the mall parking lot across from the Hotel. Turn in the next driveway." This was different then back in Detroit the police usually didn't show up for hours. These police are out here like it was a riot. Dom must have notice my far away thoughts. "This is a rich neighborhood they try to keep the piece down here. Do you think anyone saw us leaving the scene?" He asked. "Dom you should always look at your surroundings when you doing dirt. I didn't see anybody around when I fired my gun. The side street was deserted. We were walking away when people started to gather." "Which way should I go?" "My car is right there on the left." Dom pulled up next to my car and put the car in park. "Look Dom, Thank you for the dresses, but I don't think I'm ready for all this. I don't think I can

65

separate the lady you want and the woman that works for you." I said. "Keysha I'm really feeling you and I need you around me. I want you as my business partner and my life partner. Shit I can't decide either. I lay at night and think about you. Then I think about how down to earth you are. I never met anyone like you. It's like you put some sort of trance over me. I don't know what to do. But I'm willing to try anything to be in your presence." "Dom, I thought I would never even look at a man outside my race. When you kissed me in the warehouse I lost my cool. I'm usually in control of my emotions. But around you I melt. I don't think I can love another man because I'm still in love with the man I lost. I just want to be upfront with you." He moved closer to me in the car and said. "Keysha I'm not rushing you all I want you to do is have an open mind." He leaned over touched my face and gently kissed my lips. I think he was trying to see my reaction. I opened my mouth and accepted his hot lips. I pushed my tongue to meet his as we exchange the hot saliva that made us one. My passion for lust was spilling out of the pores of my body. His passion for me was evident by the hot moans coming from him as we kissed for twenty minutes. His hand slid under my shirt and gripped my breast. The wetness in my pants was pouring out. I couldn't give him myself on the first date. He felt me tense up with my thoughts. He grabbed my hand and put it on his thigh. I slowly moved my hand up his thigh while his tongue infiltrated the inner parts of my mouth. His breath was like a fresh breeze that had me sucking on his tongue to get the taste. My body was shaking and when I felt that huge hard dick that felt so big I had to open my eyes. When I pulled away my cell phone rang. We both came out of our little intimate moment. I looked at the phone and it was Cye with a 999 call. That meant an emergency. I answered before I could say hello Cye said. "Tee you all right they had a news flash that some people got killed in downtown LA. I know you went downtown I was worried." "I'm alright girl. I'll be home in an hour. Dom and I are just chilling." "That sounds good tell Dom I said what up" Cye said. "My girl said what's up Dom, I holler at you soon, bye. Dom I got to go. I really enjoyed your company. About earlier we got some things to talk about." "Tomorrow Keysha, I want to remember this beautiful day we had together. I'll call Key tomorrow." He smiled and kissed me goodbye. I got out of his car and got in mine. He waited until I pulled off them followed me out of the parking structure. I waved bye and saw his lights in my rear view mirror turn at the next red light.

Mama Raised A Killer II

Chapter 8   Making My Enemy Gullible

When I arrived home Cye had a lot of questions. She looked at me and said "you are glowing did you give him some." "No I didn't but dam Cye, he had me wetting my panties. He is so romantic. He treated me like a real queen." "White boy got you sprung already, Tee don't get caught up we on a mission." She said. "I know sis, trust me know one will stop us from our mission especially not a man." I thought about the bags I left in the car. "I forgot something in the car I'll be right back." I went and retrieved the bags from the car and threw them on Cye's lap. "What is this, Dom bought these for you? This is almost ten thousand dollars worth of dresses the still got the price tags on them. Tee. You must have gave him some pussy some head or something." Cye said while laughing and looking

69

at the dresses. "Which one is mine" "You can have any two, I was thinking about you when I tried them on." "For real Tee" she was so exited she just started taking her clothes off to try on the dresses. I sat down and enjoyed the way Cye looked so happy. I thought about a few months ago when I found her on the street. She has made so much progress. I smiled and again vowed to myself that nothing or nobody will stop us from getting revenge for our parents and the suffering of our life's that were affected. "Cye you look so beautiful in that dress you going to hurt somebody." We both laughed. After she finished trying on the dresses we sat down and talked. I told her what happened, every detail of my day with Dom. We also talk about our mission and I assured her that I will always stay focus. It was about four o'clock in the morning before we finally went to bed. I think we both missed the long talks we use to have. The only missing ingredient was mama. I feel a sleep crying softly thinking about my mother and being without my own child.

The next morning Dom called again at 11 o'clock on the dot. I think he has a thing for punctuality. He asked us to meet him at the house we first meet in Compton. I told him we would be there by 2 o'clock. Cye and I got dressed we dressed down in blue jeans gym shoes and big shirts. I couldn't believe Cye actually dressed down I couldn't get her to do that years ago. I guess now for us every day is a mission. We met Dom at the house. When he opened the door there were six guys in there looking at us funny. I could tell that they were users by the look in their eyes. "This is Key and Cece, these are my partners. I do not mean workers I said partners. So if you fuck up our money you will have to deal with them and I promise you, you don't want that. This is Eric, Jerome, Jay, Donnie, JB and Ton." Dom said. "Hi" I said, "What's up" Cye said. "Ok, this is the deal. I will have three houses that will be run by you six guys. This house will be the money drop off house only.

There will never be any product here. I'll give each house a cell phone only to be used to call for a money drop when you out of product or if you have a problem. I don't fore see any problems. When you call for a drop off someone will meet you here. One person will come the other stays at the house. We won't have more than one drop off at a time. Remember I pay some of the police so don't get any ideas any questions?" Eric said, "Where do we get the product from." "You will pick up your product and be responsible for getting it to your house. If you get jacked you pay for it. I know everything about each one of you, your mama's your daddy's and your brothers, sisters and kids. So don't play with us. If you don't want to be a part of this you can leave and never come back. If you down come back here in two hours to get your first package. You ladies have any questions for these gentlemen or anything to say?" Cye said "No" I said "I do, Don't try to play us, we will not take any shorts and don't try to skim off the top of the package. That's it" "And please don't take us for granted" Cye chimed in. "Here are your phones if I don't call you before five o'clock I'll meet you here. Alright you can leave now." Dom said as he went to the door and opened it. All the men left the house. "We need to talk" Dom said. "Dam, Keysha you look good even when you trying not to" "Oh, I'm Keysha now" I said. We both laughed Cye didn't get it. "You ladies know I got all this product that I'm not suppose to have. I told my connection I got jacked and I told my family I got jacked. All eyes will be on me to see if I'm moving all this weight. That's where you ladies come in. I need you to be my partners. I know this is a lot for you, but the rewards is half of all the profit. That could be a lot of money. If my connect gives me the product back or my money, then everything is profit. If not as long as I get my 250k back half is still yours. That may seem like a lot, but this is California and most of my cliental are millionaires. I think we should be finish with this package in sixty days. What you ladies think?" "It looks like we are going to be taking all the risk." I said. "If you're not around, nobody going to trust us." "I will always be around I'll be in the background. I'll bring the product for you to distribute and they will bring you the money and I'll be there." "Suppose we have some conflict and we will." Cye asked. "Then we will deal with it. I have some soldiers but their loyalty is to the drugs. You need to find someone you can build some trust in and we all can make lots of money." "How much money will we make" Cye asked. "The package should bring in 1.5 million. If I somehow get my money back or they replace my package, that's .5 million each. If not you should get about 375k. How does that sound?" Dom asked. "Dom we are not staying in Cali for too long, this might be a one time thing. Can you handle that" I asked. "I should hope to change your mind" he said looking directly at me. "You might change her mind but not mind I have to leave in a few months, my parents are sick." Cye said. "I will not leave my sister again Dom, you must understand that. If not we walk now." We both got up to leave. "Hold on ladies, I will just have to deal with that. With half a million dollars each where ever you go, you will be happy." He said. "Now let's get this product separated and to these houses. We will drop each off at the houses so you will know where they are. This will be the only time you should have to handle any product. You are to make sure the money is right and make sure we don't have any problems." After getting all the houses started Dom wanted to go out but Cye and I declined. Dom pulled me to the side and asked me if we could hang out. I told him not tonight we had to get our mind set for the next day. Things took off. The next few weeks went by fast. Cye and I could not believe that this much drugs was sold in this rich California area. We hadn't forgotten about our mission. We decided that we could make the money and get deeper in the organization. Our job was to get the money from the house after the drop off keep it until we see Dom. I hired Dave the first guy I meet in Cali. I used him to get me hooked up

75

with Dom. I keep him at the drop spot only the days of drop off. I paid him well and he stayed high which made him loyal to me. I also got him a little apartment and a hoopty (An old raggedy car). I also had him put my car in his name and told him when we leave he could have it. Everything went smooth for the first 30 days or so. This particular day I woke up with a knot in my stomach. Cye and I showered and dressed then headed for the drop spot. Both of us had our usual arsenal of weapons. Cye had her two glocks and I had my two pearl handle nine millimeters. This day I grabbed my 380 and stuck it in the small of my back. Our usual procedure was to go to the house call the person who wanted to drop their money off then wait for the drop off. The workers would come in the house and Dave would search them then bring them in the dining room so Cye could count the money in front of them while I stayed on guard. We called Eric to meet us at the house. As soon as we got inside the house the door bell rang. Dave answered the door and said it was Eric. When he entered

Jay came in with him. "Hold on, what you doing here?" I asked. "Jay said "We waiting for product. I called Dom he said make my drop." "Cye get both the drops and I'll call Dom." I called Dom and got his voice mail. Dave had a shot gun on his lap pointed in the direction of Eric who stood next to him. When Jay came over to put his drop on the table I turned to call Dom again. In an instant Jay drew a gun and put it to Cye's chest. When Dave raised his shot gun Eric pulled a gun and shot Dave hitting his shoulder. "Ok Miss Key" Jay said. Put your guns on the table. One at a time I know you carry two. If not I'll blow this bitches head off." Dave was hollering in pain. Cye's eyes were on me like she was ready to go for her gun and die waiting on me to give her the go ahead. "Alright relax, Dave you ok?" I asked while pulling my guns from my purse. "I'm ok, Key just losing a lot of blood." He said. "You lucky I didn't dead your punk ass." Eric said. "We just want the money" Jay put the gun to Cye's head and told her to put her gun on the table. Cye always kept a gun taped under the table just in case. She took the gun out of her purse and put in on the table. "He smacked Cye with his other hand causing her to fall to the floor. "Where is your other gun." He asked. "I don't have but one, you wanna search me." She unbuttoned her blouse reveling her big 34D firm titties, she never wore bras. "I might want to do that" he said with lust in his eyes as Cye got off the floor. "Get the money Jay that's what we came here for." My instinct told me that they were going to kill us. They had the money when they came in. They could have easily just not showed up. They going to kill us and take the money and go back to work to make it look like an inside job. "Where is the other gun hot mess?" Jay's mind was on his other head. "Turn around let me search you" Jay said. "Grab the money and let's go" Eric said moving closer to Jay. "She got another gun, I want to search her man" Jay said. He smacked Cye again and turned her around facing the table. He started to feel on her chest as though he was searching. He patted her down on her sides and back. Cye had on a skirt so he reached under her skirt, Cye never wore any underwear and his hand hit a wet moist pussy. It was so soft he didn't want to bring his hand up. His finger found the spot. Erik was looking at him smiling and didn't notice Cye reach under the table and pulled the gun out. With one motion she slapped his hand from under her skirt with one hand, then spun around and shot him in the head with the gun in her other hand. The second Eric saw the gun blast he couldn't react fast enough before I pulled my 380 automatic from my back and shot twice hitting him in the chest and forehead. His body hit the floor with a thump. Dave was almost in shock. We needed to get him to a hospital or kill him and leave him here. "They were going to kill us Tee, I mean Key" Cye said forgetting my alias for a minute. "Let's think for a minute. Dave knows better than to let more than one person in at a time." I said. "You're right he let both of them in. You think he is part of it." Cye asked while walking over to Dave. Dave was fading in and out I went and got some towels and put pressure on his wound. "Dave, you can live or die right now. I could take you to the hospital or I can leave you here to die. Now tell me are you part of this?" I asked. Dave started coughing as Cye put her gun to his head. "Naw Key I wouldn't hurt you" "So why you let Eric and Jay in and you didn't search them and you know we only allow one person in at a time. Why?" I asked like I was concern. "Ok sis you can go ahead and do him" Cye cocked her gun ready to pull the trigger. "Wait Key, Dom came by before you got here and told me to let both of them drop and they were cool." "What, let's kill him he going to tell Dom he told us." Cye said. "Key no, I'm your boy I was set up too, they was going to kill me too. I know they wouldn't have let me walk." "I think he's right. If we take you to the hospital you tell Dom that you didn't tell us nothing. Ok" I asked. Cye removed the towel on his wound and put her gun where the bullet was and pressed it real hard. "Do you understand us, we helped you so much I'm so hurt I should kill you" I said. "Key I swear to God, I'll tell him what you want, I owe you. Please take me to the hospital." Dave asked. "Go get in your car, I'll drive you and sis will follow us." Dave left and went and started his car. "Should we call Dom, Tee" Cye asked. "Naw let's wait for him to call let's see how this play's out. Get the money Cye." I drove Dave to the hospital parked his car and gave him the keys. "Dave I don't want to come looking for you" I said. "Key I'll be back to work as soon as you need me. I'm in your corner, please believe me. I'll prove it to you, Thanks." Dave walked to the emergency and Cye and I pulled off. We decided to go get something to eat. Since we were in Compton we stopped at a restaurant on the way back home. We must really be getting to be hard nose killers. How we can kill someone then go eat is beyond me. We needed something to stop our adrenaline. Cye wanted some coffee and I needed some tea. We didn't eat we had to think. "If Dom is in the middle of this he might know who we are. Then we will be set up eventually." I said talking to Cye but really thinking out loud. "Maybe

81

he was at the drop waiting on you and got a call and had to leave. Then he told Dave everything is cool not knowing about the stick up." Cye answered. "If he didn't know then why didn't he answer his phone." "he could have been getting busy, you won't give him none." Cye said trying to lighten our tension. "Seriously we almost got blown away and we haven't reached our goal. Cye, we here back in the game and we are no closer to find the killers of our parents. We need to change our tactics. Let's get out of here we need to go home and put a plan together." "I need to get this money together for your boy anyway." We had so much money we were beginning to get careless. We should have took that drop money home first. After we left the restaurant we turned the corner walking towards the car. I saw a man leaning on the car smoking on the passenger side. Cye said "We getting jacked, they trying to steal our car." "Hey, that's my car" I said. The lookout man stood straight up and said hurry up to his accomplice. As we ran to the car Cye had her gun out. The guy under the wheel jumped up and took off running. The lookout guy tried to be hard and looked at me and laughed while he backed away. Cye let off a couple of rounds in his direction and he ran away ducking and hollering like a little bitch. Our steering column was broke but we could still use the key. "The money, where is it?" Cye asked. I dug under the passenger seat and found the bag. Cye and I looked at each other and started laughing. The thought of the thieves working so hard to steal the car and over forty thousand dollars was under the seat. We road in silence both deep in thought until my cell phone rang. It was Dom. "Hello" I answered. "He Key you count up yet, what's my take?" he asked. I just looked at the phone trying to find an answer. "We had an issue at the house you need to go clean it up call me later." Then I hung up. I didn't let him ask any question. He called back over and over again for the next ten minutes. Then I guess he arrived at the house and found his answer. When we got home Cye and I went to our rooms. I got in the tub with candles and soaked. I took a bubble bath. I found myself touching my body a little more than usual. I masturbated with myself thinking about the man's hand under Cye's skirt and thinking about Dom's kisses and his hands on my body. I climaxed when I pictured that big dick of Dom that I felt through his pants. I finish bathing lotion myself down and laid down for an hour. I met Cye downstairs in the kitchen eating some fruit. My phone had eight messages on it from Dom.

Mama Raised A Killer II

Chapter 9

Sleeping With The Enemy

Cye and I went in the living room where she had all these papers with numbers. She had the money stacked up in three piles. "Ok Teeka, we have $125,000. Dollars each and Dom has 125K also. We have $250,000 in a safe deposit vault that we already had. We made half a million dollars in forty days." She said. "Cye none of that money will do us any good if we dead. I have a plan you down with it?" "Tee I told you we're a team. Whatever you do I got your back." "Dom has been blowing my phone up. I'm going to make him wait until we get our plan together. We are not going to get caught up like that again." I picked up my phone and dialed a number. Hello the person said we they picked up. "What's up cous?" I said. Who this the person asked. "This is your cousin Teeka" Cye looked at me strange she would know any relatives I had. She knew I didn't have any but her sister. She kept her ears open listening to my every word. "I'm fine" I said. I moved into another room so I could talk in private. "Reggie, you told me I could call you when I needed you." I said "What's wrong Tee somebody hurt you" Reggie asked. "I'm in California with my cousin. I can't talk on the phone. Can you come spend some time with us until we get control of this situation?" I asked. "How long Tee should I drive up" he asked. "Reggie I need you to fly and bring at list two of you loyal friends that don't mind putting in work. They might have to stay couple of months. I will take care of all expenses and you would make 100k if things go right." "Tee give me time to set up and I'll be there in three days is that cool" "Fine Reggie, call me when you ready and I'll pick you up at the airport. Thank you, see you soon." "Teeka, I told you I will always be there for you, I'll call you, Bye." I hung up and returned to the living room. Cye was standing there with her hands on her hips. "Were you talking to my sister?" she asked. "Naw Cye I was talking to Reggie, you remember him Carl's cousin." "Yes I remember him." "I called to Detroit to get us some backup. I have a plan and we should be out of this town one way or the other in three months." I said. What's the plan Cye asked. I broke it down to her she agreed and disagreed with some parts. We both agreed on the mission. After hours of talking we both fell asleep on the sofa's. It was a long day. My phone woke me up around three o'clock in the morning. It was Dom. I wanted to make him wait but I had to get a feel if he set us up before Reggie got there. "Hello Dom, What's up?" "Dam girl why you didn't answer my calls? I didn't know if you were hurt or if someone kidnapped you. You had me worried." He said. "Well I didn't know if you set us up or not and I still don't know" I screamed. "What? Why would you think that?" "Because Dave said you ok'd them guys to come together." "Jay called me and said he had too much money over at the house I told him to drop it off. I was there but I had to leave. Look I can't talk over the phone can you meet me for lunch later?" "I don't know call me later, did you clean up the house?" Yes, but we got to move, I'll call you later. Hope you are alright." He hung up and I went back to sleep."

I woke to the smell of breakfast being cooked by Cye. I went and showered and brushed my teeth. Put on a robe and went down to eat breakfast with Cye. "What's the agenda for today Tee?" "We having lunch with Dom I want you to see if you can read him. Get a fill to see if he was involved." "That's cool, dress up or down." She asked. "Sexy" I said "we going to change our tactics be ready about one." At 12:30 Cye was downstairs looking like she stepped out of a fashion magazine. She had gained her weight back, her hair was flawless. Her makeup was perfect and she was dressed to kill. "Dam Cye, who are you going to meet looking that good?" We both laughed. Dom had called at his usual 11:00 o'clock and I arrange for me and Cye to meet him downtown at 1 o'clock. He picked a quiet restaurant that was almost empty so we could talk. When we walked into the restaurant all heads turned. I must admit we were looking good. I decided to wear one of the dresses Dom bought for me. It fit me good and showed all the curves my body could afford to show. We were getting looks from the two couples on each side of the restaurant and all the staff, women and men. Dom saw us and signaled for us to join him. "You ladies look beautiful I am honored to grace the same room as you. Let alone have the pleasure of dinning with you. "Thanks Dom, I needed that" Cye said. "Hi Dom, you look handsome yourself." "I cleaned house, so what happened the other day?" he asked. "We will never be caught with our panties down again. We don't know if we were set up or that your crew is not loyal to you and tried to set you up." I said. "Here is your take for the last 40 days is 125k. We both got the same. Cye said pushing a small leather bag to Dom." "My sister and I are thinking about moving on. Even though the money is good, the risk of our life's mean more to us." "Wait hold on a minute. I don't know what or how that went down but it will never happen again." Dom said. "We don't know if you were a part of it or not, but I don't like to be slapped around." Cye's mind set was different. She pulled her gun from her purse cocked it at put it under the table and said. "Dom keep your hands on the table where I can see them. I really believe you had something to do with this, but unless you can convince me otherwise, my sister and I will be the only ones walking out of here today." "Hold on Cece" I said. "What the fuck is this, Key I'm trying to trust you guys, but you got to trust me too. I just want to find out who is behind this shit. Look I came to also tell you ladies that I got the product replaced and as we agreed and that makes your profit more." Dom said. "It ain't about no money Dom, what the fuck we need money for if we can't spend it." "Whatever you want to do I'm down with it. We are in this together. I need both of you, but you got to trust me." Dom was beginning to almost beg. The look in Cye's eyes was death. She wanted to kill him right now while she had a chance. "Sis, let's think about this for a minute. You know whatever you do I got your back. We haven't reached our goal. We need that money for your sick parents. Come on girl, put the gun down. We will handle things our own way now. Is that cool with you Dom?" Dom had to agree so reluctantly Cye put the gun back in her purse without taking her eyes off Dom. "Everybody is a little tense. We need to relax a little. We ordered some food and everybody ate in silence. After lunch Dom said. "I got the perfect idea. They have a red carpet gathering at the Kodak Theatre a few miles away. We should go you ladies want to go? I don't hold any grudges. I'm trying to build the trust between us. We can hang out with the stars and you ladies look like you belong with them. Would you like that?" Cye looked and me and our eyes said hell yes. "Yes we can do that" I said. "Keysha, Cece no more business until tomorrow and I apologize for what happen. I promise

I will find out who set us up. So let me take you ladies out on the town. Enjoy the day relax a little." "Ok" we agreed and for the next few hours we went shopping, went to a special screening of a movie. I was around all these celebrities. Cye and I felt good, this did a lot to boost our confidence. In the evening we walked the red carpet at the Kodak and people thought we were celebrities. They kept taking pictures asking us who were our agents. It was a fantastic night. Dom was a great host. He knew everybody. "After everybody was leaving, Dom asked if he could stop by his house before he dropped us at our car. We agreed as we both thought that we need to know where he lives so we can get closer to our goal of completing our mission. We drove for a while and talked about the funny acting celebrities. I notice the sign read Huntington Park. The streets were cleaned as we pulled up in a beautiful neighborhood. I didn't see any cars this sometimes tells you how influential the area is. To my surprise everybody owns large garages and no one parks on the street. Dom pushed his garage opener and we pulled into an eight plus car garage. With all different kinds of luxury cars in it a Porsche, a Bentley, Benz, BMW and a few more I couldn't name. When we got out Dom noticed the shocked look on our faces. These are my dad's and my uncle's cars. My dad use to stay here but I took over because he's down for a while. We took an elevator up to the third floor. When we got out the house was beautiful. We could see the two floors below as we walked around the vestibule. The family room where he took us was decorated in a modern design. Expensive art hung on the walls. The biggest television I ever saw, when he hit a button on the remote soft music came from every angle of the room. We sat on the couch and fell deep into to soft cushion. The fire place was as big as the television and it too turned on with a remote. We looked around enjoying the scenery when Dom asked as if we wanted a drink. We had already had a couple and I was feeling pretty good. I know Cye had her buzz on. We both said yes. He then pushed another button on his remote and the wall came down and the glass bar pushed out with everything you think you wanted to drink. He mixed us a martini and we had a toast to our future. "We must have each other's back and trust each other" Dom said. We touched glasses and drank to our new alliance. I was all smiles because I was feeling we were getting closer to the family. I also think that Dom's father is Mark Gucci the person charged with killing our parents. I think Cye must have sensed something too. She was giggling and dancing to the music all sexy. She kept looking at me and then at Dom as though she wanted my approval. As I said we are getting so close that I will do anything to complete our mission. After a couple more drinks Dom and Cye were buzzed and started dancing together. Dom said "Come on Keysha join us." I got up and started feeling the music also. Cye started to undue her cloths. By the next song both of us were in our underclothes. "Dom come on and join us." I asked. Dom took his shirt and pants off revealing his hard erection. Cye and I stood there amazed at how large he was. Cye danced over to him and turned her butt around and rode his hard dick with her butt. I went to his back and started kissing on his neck. I put my arms around his waist and grinded to the beat of the music from behind him. I could see how turned on his was. He was moving with his eyes closed like he was in a dream and didn't want to wake up. My body was sweating and my insides were wet. My panties were wet also. I took them off. I grabbed Dom's hand and put his hand on my wet pussy. His finger felt the inside walls of my vagina. I was feeling his nipples with my other hand. I looked down to see Cye pulling his pants down and inserting his huge dick in her mouth. Dom eyes were getting bigger and he was losing control. He laid down on the plush carpet while he pulled me close to him and instructed me to sit on his face. I felt his warm lips on my inner thigh. I jerked slightly as his hot tongue went deep inside my pussy. I moaned to each lick of his tongue until I climaxed on his face. Cye took off her panties while still holding and rubbing his big white dick. It looked like an ice cream stick and Cye must have thought so too because she was sucking, gagging and licking for a while. After making me climax he pushed me off of him and looked into my eyes and said "Keysha I want you let's go to the bedroom I got some rubbers up there." That was the magic word I liked him but I wasn't doing nothing if he didn't have any protection. I don't want no baby by a Gucci that I know is going to die. We went down the hall to the bedroom we were high and feeling good. Cye fixed her another drink and joined us. Dom laid me down on the bed after he put the rubber on he tried to put that big dick inside me. "It hurts Dom, take it slow. I only had a couple of men in my life none that dam big. It was really hurting. Cye stood next to me seeing the pain I was in. After a few minutes seeing me being tortured with that big dick Cye laid on the bed next to me and pulled Dom towards her. "Let me have some big daddy" she said. Dom took what little he had in me out and inserted his manhood into Cye. Cye moved a little and then she put her legs up higher and grabbed Dom and pulled him closer to her. Dom pushed his thick dick inside her and she took every inch of it. She looked into his eyes while moving her body. Dom couldn't take it he was about to cum. All that and he couldn't last more than three minutes. He started to shake and spit came out his mouth and dropped down on Cye's chest as he came all inside his rubber. "Dam" she said. Cye was frustrated and Dom could sense it. He came to fast she didn't get hers. Dom got up and laid Cye on the bed and started eating her wet pussy. For twenty minutes Cye moaned and finally begin to shake. She squeezed his head between her legs and yelled out a cry of ecstasy. Dom rolled over and fell straight to sleep. Cye and I looked at each other for a few minutes not believing we just did this to the son of the man that killed our parents. I motioned for her to follow me to the bathroom. When we got in there I asked her if she was alright. I told her I was going to look around so she should keep an eye on Dom to make sure he doesn't wake up. I went down the hall and looked in the other bedrooms. They were clean and no pictures or clothes in the closet. I snuck downstairs and looked in the other bedrooms I didn't see anything. I went down on the first floor and into the living room it was spacious. There were pictures on the wall. I begin to tremble a little when I saw John and George Gucci in a picture with three other young men. They all looked like brothers. I saw more pictures of their mother and father with Dom and what could be his father Mark Gucci. I saw pictures of little kids with each family. Then I saw a picture of Dom a little kid and the girl who had set him up. I had seen enough. I went back upstairs without touching anything. When I reached the room Dom was sitting up in the bed. "Keysha you didn't bring my clothes." Cye said. Dom looked at me empty handed. "I was trying to find some water or juice my sugar is kicking up" I said. "I'll get you something" Dom said. I turned around and went to get the clothes. Dom went to the bathroom then out the room. He returned with a picture of juice and a couple a glasses. I drank the juice and asked where can I shower. He showed me the bath and where to get towels. I showered and Cye showered in another bedroom. Dom went downstairs and I guess he showered down there because when he came back he was fully dressed. I know you guys ready for me to take you back. We got to get busy tomorrow and I have to get some product ready. We rode back listening to the music and talking about the beautiful day we had. When we reached our car Dom said "Keysha let me holler at you for a minute" Cye got out and I gave her the keys to start the car up. "What's up Dom" "Keysha I really dig you and I am sorry for what happen tonight I was caught up in the moment. I never had two women before. I just want to let you know that you are the one I want. I'm really feeling you." He said. "Dom don't sweat it, me and sister is cool. We're down with each other. I do like you Dom everything is cool." I said as I opened the car door. "But you're going to have to take it slow with me with that tool you carrying down there." I smiled and he said "I will baby" I got out got in the car with Cye and we drove off.

Mama Raised A Killer II

Chapter 10

Someone to Watch My Back

Cye was silent on the ride home. When she arrived she went upstairs and took a shower she was in there for over an hour. I pulled my thoughts together and went to bed. The next morning I woke up at eight. Cye was already up drinking coffee in the kitchen. When I came down I asked her to roll with me to take care of our own business. She said cool because she had to put some money in the safe deposit vault and see wanted me to sign in case something happen to her. We went to the bank. Then we went to pay for an apartment I had rented and also pick up the keys. The apartment was two doors from ours. We also went to buy a car. Cye picked out a triple black BMW with tented windows. She pulled the salesman outside and told him she would pay cash and give him an extra three thousand if he could get my plates and put the car in a dummy corporation. Cash he said he knew he would make a good commission. He also knew he could add some thousands on top for himself. We got the car and Cye drove it home and put it in the garage. I called Reggie to see what his status was. He said he will be in tomorrow night at 9:30 at LAX. When I hung up Dom called and said he had a new home. Cye and I met him at the new drop house which was in a good neighborhood. It looked too good to be used only for dropping off money. Dom met us there driving that Bentley that was in his garage. He had on a suit and tie he looked good. He looked like a cool Robin Thicke. Dom wanted me to hang with him but I told him Cye and I had plans. He looked so disappointed. I kissed him on the cheek and told him I'll call him later. Cye and I got in my car and left. We went and bought three beds and a living room and dining room set. I paid the company extra to have it delivered tomorrow. Dom called and said he had a couple of money drops. I asked him to handle it and told him we will be available day after tomorrow. He was mad "Shit what am I suppose to do" he asked. "You have your loyal crew, see how loyal they are. Cye is visiting her parents and I'm going with her we'll be back." I said. "Keysha you are not leaving me are you, what about our plans. I told my grandparents about you they want to meet you." "Dom, sweetheart I'll be back you can take me where you want and do what you want to me. Of course after we handle our business, we still partners." "Alright Keysha, I guess I can hold it down without you but it's going to be hard. See you soon, Bye" I said bye and he hung up. Cye and I wanted to clean the apartment and get some essentials for the boys. The next day the furniture arrived and Cye and I put our women's touch on the apartment. It was ready for the guys to crash for a couple of months. Cye and I stayed their overnight we both slept like babies. The next morning we went home showered and took care of our personal hygiene and changed clothes. Cye wanted to go the grocery store. I asked her to sit down so we can talk before the guys came. "Cye we must not forget what we are here for" I said. "Tee you don't have to remind me. You don't have to ever worry about anybody coming between us again." She said. "I love you and we should be out of this town in a couple of months. Dom wants to introduce me to his grandparents. So we are getting closer to the family and our plan will come together when the guys get here. The only thing I didn't tell you about is what I said to Reggie. I told him I'll give him 100k out my money when the job is complete." I said. "That's cool, if we get out alive I'll give 100k too. The other guys can split it up. Tee it's not about the money I just want closer at any cost. Please understand that whatever we have to do I'm down with it. I love you too Tee, you are the sister that I always wanted to be close to." She said. I got to go I'm going to cook a big meal. You have to go over to the apartment and wait for the furniture to be delivered. She grabbed her keys and left.

Mama Raised A Killer II

Chapter 11   Businessmen Or Killers

We were at the airport at nine o'clock. The plane didn't arrive until 9:30. We were excited to see the guys. At least see people we knew and of course someone down with us to give us more strength. Have our back. The plane arrived and Reggie was the first one off the plane. He must have been in first class. He saw me and smiled. He looked good he was dressed in a business suit shirt and tie. Behind him was a big white guy with a business suit on. Two brothers followed in business suits. So many people got off the plane with suit on I thought it was a convention. Reggie walked over to me and hugged my right off the floor. "Reggie the last time I saw you I was being carried in your arms. Put me down." I'm sorry Tee I'm just happy to see you alive. I heard you got killed in a fire" he smiled. "I never did thank you, thanks" I said. "I'm sorry you remember my cousin Cye" "Sure I do, I must say you look more beautiful today then the last time I saw you." He took her hand and spun her around. "Dam I always thought you were attractive but you have taken it to another level." "Flattery will get you everywhere you better be aware." Cye said "give me a hug." He pulled her close to him and hugged her. We were so into each other we forgot about the other guys standing around. "Oh, I'm sorry, where are my manners. This is my man Jimmy, Perk and this is Whitey. These are my enforcers and Whitey is also my attorney." Reggie said. He can get me into places I couldn't get into. He also knows how to invest our money. Just in case you are wondering he has a black daddy so don't let the good looks fool you. He is as deadly as all of us." We all laughed. Everybody spoke to each other then I said let's get out of here. As we walked out the airport to the car I pulled Reggie back to talk to him privately. "Reggie I need to tell you what's going on I don't want to talk in front of your crew." "It's cool Tee, these guys aren't my crew" he said. "You said they were your enforcers" I said. "They are my enforcers because that's their role. They are my partners Tee. They share equal in all the profits and everybody puts up their share to buy. Each of us has a role and we all make money. We all like making money which bonds us together. It's a win win situation. They are completely down with me as was I to Carl." The mention of Carl's name brought tears to my eyes. Reggie notice and he put his arm around my shoulder as we walked. "So I can talk freely in front of them?" I asked. "Anything you got to say to me you can say it in front of them. We've been a team for five years ever since you put me down with the game. "I never told you thanks, thanks" he said. He made me smile I forgot how funny he use to be.

I had showed the guys where we lived and told them they're always welcome. We arrived at their apartment you can smell the food before we opened the door. Cye is a very good cook. The guys couldn't believe how the apartment was laid out. "I'm sorry Reggie I only got three bedrooms because I thought you were only bringing two guys." I said. "Don't sweat it" Whitey said "one of us will always be on the couch for lookout. We been doing it that way for years" After twenty minutes Cye said let's eat. The food was good fried chicken, macaroni and cheese, yams corn bread and peach cobbler. We all ate until we were full. We drank wine and talked. They guys were talking about each other only the way true friends can. I left and went home to my apartment for a minute. I wanted to put on some comfortable clothes. When I return everybody was laughing and having a good time. Cye and Reggie seem to be bonding. "I hate to interrupt your party but we got business to handle. Everybody come in the dining room." Everybody came and sat down. "First of all I have to tell you guys what we tell you has to stay between us. Reggie says you guys are cool so I have to learn to trust you because I trust him with my life. We have a situation that we didn't ask for out here. I'm going to try to explain this and why we have to do what we are doing. This is our problem if you feel you can't put in the work you can leave tomorrow. "We all with you Tee," Perk said. "Teeka, let me explain" Cye said. "You guys know me and my cousin Tee ran the Northend and half of the mid west. Well I gave up on the life and moved to California with my mother and father. Later Tee gave up on the game and move out here to raise her daughter by Carl" "Hold up you got a daughter Tee? I have a cousin" Reggie asked. He was surprised. "Let me finish please." Cye said. Reggie you remember the Gucci brothers don't you?" "Yea, I remember who they were." Well their family came and killed my mother and father. They also killed Aunt Lolo Tee's mother and almost killed Tee's daughter Carletha." Cye started to shed tears but continue talking. "They raped my mother and tied my father up duck taped his eyes and made him watch as they violated her and killed her." Cye started crying uncontrollable. "They killed our family, they killed our family." Tears begin to form in my eyes. I went over to hug Cye. Reggie came over and hugged me. After a couple minutes of letting it out I pulled myself together. Wiping my face I said. "This is the deal. We got back in the game through our research and creativity. Our partner is Dom Gucci the nephew of the man accused of killing our parents. We have made over 375k in 3 months. All the rich people out here use cocaine. So our mission is to revenge our parents the money is icing on the cake. We won't leave until that's done. We want their whole family. We have been waiting patiently and we are getting so close. Dom calls his self liking me because he thinks I saved his life. So he trusts us. We need back up because we were set up and almost got killed. We don't know who to trust. We need help." "Tee whatever you need I'll help you. Even if it means my life for yours I'm down." Reggie said. "I'm in all the way" Perk said. Jimmy said I'm in. Whitey said "I'm down all the way I have to protect my investment" everybody laughed. This guy was cool. The fact that he was white and let people call him whitey meant a lot. I pulled out four envelopes. "This is half of the money you make. There was twenty five thousand for the guys and fifty thousand for Reggie. You will get the same when we leave. Our goal is 60 days. If we reach our goal before then we can leave. We are about to turn this town upside down. The police here respond very fast so whatever you do remember that." I said thanks to everybody. "We're going home. We got plans for tomorrow so be ready about ten o'clock." Cye got up and hugged everybody and said goodnight. We were walking out the door Reggie and Jimmy were right behind us. "We'll be alright" I said. "You will never be by yourself in these streets again while we're here." Jimmy said. They walked us to the door while watching their surroundings. I was feeling secure. I leaned over and kissed Reggie on the check. "Thanks Goodnight."

The next morning the guys were at the front door at 10 o'clock. Cye and I were waiting down stairs ready to go. Cye called all the guys in the bedroom and showed them our arsenal. "Dam ladies are we going to war." Perk said smiling. He ran to get something he liked before someone else got it. "This is me" he said holding a 45 millimeter. "This just came out." Every body found something they liked. "You need to pick two. Cye and I always double up" I said. Everybody picked another gun and each person grabbed a bullet proof vest." I told them to follow me to the garage. Once inside I gave Reggie the keys to the BMW. "This is yours Reggie I got a special job for you and Whitey. This cutlass is for doing work. No one has seen these cars. They are not in my name so if you have to leave them to save your ass it's ok. The first thing we going to do is get closer to the family. This week we are going to post up just in case we are set up again. Jimmy and Perk you guys will go with us to the drop house. Reggie you and Whitey will be close by. We need you watching our back just in case someone has the nerve to stick us up. You guys get our cell numbers. One more thing we use aliases so no one knows our real name and put two and two together. I am Key and Cye name is Cece. So don't say our names. I hope you don't think I am trying to control you guys I just know the plan. I'm sure you will do your own thing once you feel where things are going. I ain't trying to hurt your manly egos by telling you what to do." I said. "Tee it's not like that we all understand." Jimmy said. We made it to the drop house and I called Dom again I had talked to him this morning. He said he had three drops. It was the first of the month and all the celebrities got paid. He also said he purposely didn't pick up the drops so he could see how loyal his other crew is. He also said he would come by. I told him no because if they see him they might not do what they wanted. I told him I had some backup. Perk stood at the front door. Jimmy and I stayed in the dining room with our guns out. Within ten minutes there was a knock on the door. Cye went to the door and recognized Donnie. He's cool he told Perk. Jimmy walked to the door as Donnie was coming in. He grabbed Donnie and threw him against the wall. Cye and I had our guns out not knowing what was going on. Perk's gun was at Donnie's head while Jimmy searched him hard. He's clean he said. Perk put his gun down and said go in the dining room. Jimmy followed Donnie closely seeing that he was nervous. "Where is your drop" Jimmy asked. Donnie took the paper bag out of his pocket and threw it on the table. He was shaking when he pulled out a cigarette to relax himself. "No fucking smoking in here" Jimmy said. Cye counted the money and asked "How many drops are you suppose to have." "I suppose to have two, I gave one to Dom" Jimmy smacked Donnie on the back of his head with the gun. "Your drops suppose to come here nowhere else, we understand each other." Donnie rubbing the knot on his head said "yea man." "I'm calling Dom" I said going with the flow. "If you lying you got a problem, if he doesn't answer his phone you got a problem." I dialed Dom's number it was tense in the house. Everyone was on alert. The phone kept ringing. I let it ring a few more times looking straight at Donnie. I hung up the phone. Jimmy and Perk cocked their guns and moved toward Donnie. "Wait a minute I ain't lying" he yelled. My phone rung everybody froze. It was Dom "Hello, Dom Donnie is here saying you picked up a drop from him. You told me to pick up all drops." I said. "Key, I got the drop he had too much money for me to let him hold it." Dom said. "Look Dom if I'm getting the drops then let me deal with that. I'm not going to be going back and forth. We pick up all drops from this point on alright." "Ok Key" he said. Then I hung up the phone. I had to let everybody know we were still in control. "He's cool, let him get out of here." I told the guys. After two more drops we all left. Reggie and Whitey were still posted up outside until we left. I contemplated counting the money in front of the guys. But I had to see if they were going to be part of this team. I hope that we would not have any problems between us. We went back to the house ate drank wine and talked. It was really good having some friendly faces around again. Dom kept trying to get with me and I keep putting him off. I only saw him when we met to give him the money. I told him I had my cousin here helping me out but I never let him see none of the guys. The next couple of weeks went smooth. I called Reggie one evening and told him to come over I needed to talk to him. When he came over I told him I had a special project. We talked and he looked nervous. "What's up Reggie, you look worried." He looked down and said he was cool. "We family Reggie I trust you with my life. There is nothing you can tell me that we can't workout. What's up?" I asked. "Teeka I'm sorry" he said. I reached for my purse with my gun in it thinking I was getting ready to be robbed. He saw my reaction and said "Hold on Tee it ain't like that" my hand was on my gun I un cocked it inside my purse. With a hardness in my voice tone ready to go out blazing if he made the wrong move "So what you sorry for" I asked. "Tee I'm really feeling Cye. I know we family and we're on a mission, but I really like her." I jumped up with my gun out. "What the fuck," Reggie backed away trying to reach for his gun in his back. "Why you, I'm, I'm really happy for you." He looked at me to see if I was serious. I smiled and put my gun down. "I was just fucking with you. I know Cye been sneaking somewhere in the middle of the night. I thought Whitey was hitting it." He came over and lifted me off the ground and gave me a big hug. "I love you like my big sister Tee. Nothing will come between our family." He said. "I love you too Reggie, where is that hot ass Cye?" I asked. Cye came running down the stairs and hugged Reggie then hugged me. "What you think Cye, I was going to shoot you?" I asked. They both said "Yea." We all started laughing. We stayed up playing cards and talking about the old neighborhood. I went to bed and left the lovers hugging on the couch. I was truly happy for Cye.

Chapter 12

Pushing Dom Gucci's Buttons

The next day we had to pick up drops. We all went to the house and posted up as usual. After a few minutes the door bell rang. Ton came in and was searched. The word had got out that the people running the drops were killers. We hadn't had an incident since the guys arrived. Ton dropped his money and couldn't wait to get out of there. My phone rang and it was Reggie "two guys coming your way, salt and pepper." He hung up. "Perk you and Jimmy come in here quickly. The guys came in the dining room with their guns out. "What's up" they asked. I pushed Cye in the kitchen and waved for the guys to hurry up. Before we got the door closed shooting begin. I had to stop the guys from running out there. "Hold on, not yet" everybody looked at me and knew I had a plan. "Reggie is outside" Cye said. "He's alright, wait until the shooting stops then we go out." The shooting stopped and everybody ran outside with guns out only to see Dom in the bushes hiding. There was a body at the front door. I looked around and didn't see Reggie or Whitey so I knew everything went good. "Dom you ok" I asked. "Somebody tried to kill me, I bet it was them dam Mexicans" he yelled. "Get that guy in the house." I told the guys. Dom explained that he came with him. It was JB bringing his drop. He had got shot in the chest and the head. He was dead. I introduced Jimmy and Perk to Dom and told him they were my cousins. Dom was shaking saying again that someone was trying to kill him. I had thought that he would call his family. They would come get him and Reggie and Whitey could follow them and find out where they lived at. Or he would beg Cye and I to ride him to his house or to his family's home. Either way was ok with us. That means we were getting closer to his family. Dom went in the kitchen to make a phone call.

Across town two men walked up to a house with a circle driveway. There was a hard knock on the door. When the young lady peered through her half open blinds she asked "who is it" The burly white said "police, Miss we need to ask you a couple of questions. There was a shooting a couple doors down and we are talking to all the neighbors." "Hold on a minute" Tonya rushed in to hide the cocaine she was sniffing in her bedroom. She peeped in the see her son playing video games and went to answer the door. She half cracked the door to see to two large men dressed in business suits. One white and one black with badges chained around their necks. "I'm sorry to bother you Miss we just need five minutes. May we come in?" he asked so politely. Since she saw the white man she thought it was safe to let them in. "Sure but I have to take my son to the doctor in a few minutes so please hurry." The two men entered the house and was lead to the dining room. "What's this about" the lady said. Both guys pulled their guns. Before she could scream a large hand was around her mouth and the cold steal gun was against her temple. "Do not scream or I'll kill you then your son. You understand." She shook her head in agreement. "Call your son" tears formed in her eyes as she did what she was told. "DJ get down here, right now." She yelled in panic. The man moved behind her and let her feel the gun at her neck. The kid came running to the sound of his mother's panic voice. Before he could reach her the other man put a cloth around his mouth and held her son while he fail limp into his arms knocked out. "No not my son, what the fuck you want. You aren't police." She looked at the fake toy badges through tears running down her face. "Shut up" she watched the other man tie her son up and lay him on the couch. He then put his gun to the kids head and looked at Reggie for instructions. "I know you are Dom's baby mama, where is his stash" he asked rather calmly. "I don't know" was all she said before she felt the back side of the gun clash with her head. She put her hand up feeling a big knot swell bigger and bigger. Whitey took the safety off his gun and cocked it. He put it on the boys forehead as he laid there unconscious. "No" the mother screamed, "ok it's in the safe, please don't hurt my baby." Reggie yanked her up and pushed her. She lead him in the back bedroom. She opened the closet full of men's clothes. She didn't hesitate to open the safe. She didn't tell them about the drugs in the other bedroom hoping that she could keep that for herself when they leave. In the safe was a large bag full of money some stocks and bonds. Whitey gathered up everything and stuffed it in the bag. "That's it that's all he left. He just left here a couple of hours ago and he took everything else with him. Please don't hurt us." Reggie pushed her back in the dining room. Whitey went and stood over the kid put his gun to his chest. Reggie made the young lady sit down. "Now I can kill you or your son I'll let you decide." "No wait the drugs are in the closet in the other bedroom. Please don't hurt me." She said tears running down her face. Reggie shot her once in the head. Then he waved off Whitey. He was mad that she was more concern about herself then her child. Whitey went in the bedroom and found the drugs. Reggie untied the kid hands and feet, he left the knots loose enough so he could get free when he woke up. They took the drugs and money and left the house nice and neat except for the dead body.

Back at the drop house Dom called for his cleanup crew to take care of the body. He also called his uncle to let him know what was going on. His uncle was on his way. Dom returned to the dining room and informed us. While I was trying to think of a plan to get going Cye's cell phone rang. She had a surprise look on her face and she looked at me. I read her eyes as she continued her conversation in private. She came back. "Key that was the nurse I have to leave." She said. "Is everything alright" I asked. "Dad is getting worse. Are you coming with me?" She asked. "Dom we got to roll, you going to take care of everything here." Before he could answer his phone went off. His eyes got bigger as he listened to the person on the other end. Tears formed in his eyes as he whispered "Tonya is dead? Is my son alright?" His heart stood still as he waited for the answer. "Wow, where is he" he asked "I'll be right there." Dom hung up the phone and said someone had killed his baby mama and tied up his son. He wanted us to follow him to his uncle's house. To make sure he made it safe. His uncle said he would wait for Dom there. I told him Dom we only had one car and I had to go with Cye. He asked me to ride with him and keep his car to meet with Cye. "It will only take and extra fifteen minutes out your way, please Keysha I need you I need to think not drive." He pleaded. "Ok, Jimmy you ride with me and Perk you ride with Cye. You guys can follow me. After I drop off Dom we'll take the money and put it at the drop. Then we can go see your dad." I said. We closed the house down and we both drove out the driveway. I told Cye to call me and keep me posted if anything changes. Keep me close I said as we drove away. This meant to Cye and I that she should follow me and keep me at a close distances. Cye called Reggie to let him know what was going on. That is who Cye was talking to when she said her dad was sick. He told Cye what happened on his end. Dom showed me the directions to his uncle's house. Cye and Perk were following us in their car and Reggie and Whitey was following them a block behind. As we pulled up to the gated house there were two cars facing the exit. I had a nervous feeling inside. We pulled to the entrance and two guys armed with AK assault rifles meet us. They saw Dom and waved us though. When Cye pulled up behind us the other car moved backwards and blocked us in. The guys with the assault rifles stuck there guns in the car and had Perk and Cye on lock. If they moved they would be killed. The next thing I knew two more guys drew guns on me and Jimmy. I could see Jimmy getting ready to make a move for his gun. I reached to my purse and had my hand on my 9 Millimeter. "Hold the fuck up, what are you doing.

This is my crew they're protecting me." Dom yelled. Nobody moved they weren't listening to Dom. I could see in my rear view mirror that Reggie and Whitey was outside the gate. They got out the car and had their guns on the two guys with the assault rifles who had their backs to them. I probably can take this guy by surprise but I think Jimmy going to get hit. One guy had his gun to his head. Everything was moving slow. "Terry what the fuck you doing, they with me" Dom said directly to the guy standing by my window. The guy didn't answer he just picked up his phone and dialed a number. Everyone was at a standstill. "We got a situation" he said into the phone. Then he hung up. A short ball headed man came down the driveway. Looked at us then at Dom. "Uncle Chris what is this, they're with me." "Dominique you were almost assassinated. How do I know they didn't set you up" Dom's uncle Chris said. "This lady took a bullet for me a couple of months ago. She saved my life. You know I must trust her to bring her here. This is the young lady I told you about this is my partner." Dom pleaded. Uncle Chris looked at us. He looked at me a little longer than usual. Looked inside the car and noticed my hand in my purse and Jimmy's hand under the seat with his gun out. "If they had wanted me dead Uncle I would have been dead already. How is my son?" Dom asked. Uncle Chris waved his men off and before he turned around Reggie and Whitey were gone. I got out the car "nice to meet you sir Dom please call me later. Hope your son is ok." I said before I walked over to the car Cye was driving. Let's get the fuck out of here before he remembers me. We backed out the driveway as soon as his goons moved the car that had us blocked in. I could see one of them write down my license plate number. We drove off burning rubber. After a mile I looked back and Reggie was following us. The long ride home was silent. The thought of death facing you makes you think. I believe everybody was thinking sooner or later death is going to catch up with us. When we arrived at the house I told the guys we were going to shower. We will then be over to their house to talk in about an hour. I went to my room to shower and Cye did the same. We both were back down stairs in about forty minutes. We were chilling on the couch when the door bell rang. Cye ran to the door and opened it. Reggie and Whitey walked in smiling. Whitey had a two bottles of Champagne and carried a big duffle bag. "What's going on, I thought we was coming over to your house?" I asked. Reggie didn't answer he just pulled Cye and I into the dining room. Whitey opened the bags and poured its contents onto the table. My eyes got big as melons. Cye was holding her hand over her mouth. It was at lot of money and at least fifty kilos of drugs and some stocks and bonds. "Home boy was living with his baby mama and he used it as his stash house." Reggie said. "Dam" is all I could say. "I didn't tell the other guys. I figure we could work something out between the four of us." Reggie said. "My thoughts are you girls can have most of the money and we will take the drugs." Whitey said. "First let's count the money" I said. We spent the next few hours counting money and drinking Champaign. We talked about what Dom would do when he found out the money and drugs were gone. Whitey said that Dom would think the police got it since they were the first to arrive on the scene. I was beginning to feel Whitey he was so down to earth. It must be the Champaign working on me. I was looking at him differently. When we finish counting the money it totaled $1,345,050. That was a lot of money to have lying around. "What do you ladies think, Cye" Cye said the money is cool but we are here for a purpose. The drugs won't do us any good because our plans are not to get back in the game. "I got money I just want revenge and closure." Cye said. Tears begin to build in her eyes as she thought about her parents. "Look guys we have to close this up in this town. I want to go see my child and start building my life back up." I said. "You guys can take the $345,050 Thousand and split it up between all of you and you guys can keep the drugs." I said. "Anything you want Teeka." Whitey said. Reggie said "Whitey and I agreed that the stocks and bonds go to our great cousin Carletha. Is that alright with you" he asked. "Yea that's cool but the one condition Cye and I want. I want this to end in two weeks. Whatever way this is going to play out, we want to be out of California in two weeks." I said. "Can we do this Reggie you got a couple of leads? Can we make it happen so Cye and I can go back to living normal again?" "Yes we can make it happen. A lot of bodies going to fall I don't want you or Cye in the middle." Reggie said. "We already in the middle" Cye said. "I want to pull the trigger" "Alright we need to relax, here Teeka have some more Champaign." Whitey said. He poured me a glass as he continued to look into my eyes. I don't know if he was reading my mind or was I reading his. It seem like we were both on the same page. We all drank and talked until late in the morning. Cye pulled Reggie by the hand and disappeared up the stairs. I heard the door close and then I heard the ooh ah sounds. Whitey came and sat next to me on the couch and he asked me "What do you want out of life?" I was shocked. Since I had never been asked that question I didn't know how to answer it. I thought for a minute. "I just want to be happy. I want to raise my daughter in an upper class community. Away from all the violence I've been through in my life. I want to settle down and spend my life with one person." "You taking applications" he said. We both laughed. That was the ice breaker. I laid my head on his chest and he put his arms around me. He told me about his life. About his family and what he wanted in life. We talked and listen to music until I fell asleep in his arms. I must admit that was the most peaceful sleep I've had in a long time.

Chapter 13

Dope Fiend Dave Going Straight

The smell of breakfast woke me up. I looked around and saw Cye in the kitchen cooking. The chest or pillow that I felt so comfortable on was gone. "Hey where is everybody" "Reggie and Whitey got up early this morning and left. They took the drugs and said they had some business to take care of." Cye said. Since it was Sunday I decided that I would stay at home and watch TV. My phone rang it was Dom. "Hey Kee, somebody ripped me off. They took all my money and my entire product. I need to talk to you in person" Dom yelled. "Hold on Dom I've had a hard week and I'm trying to rest" "I need to talk to you, please meet me." He begged. I finally gave in. "I just got up I'll call you back in an hour." I said and hung up.

At an apartment in Compton a knock on the door is answered by a teenage girl. Two white policemen at the door made her hesitate. They asked for Dave Weston her dad. She opened the door and let them in. A hand grabbed her as she turn around to go get her dad. She felt a large gun in her back as she tried to stifle her scream. "Daddy" she yelled as the bullet silenced her scream. The sound of the scream and the gun shot brought her dad and mother running down the stairs. They stopped when the saw the guns and the two men holding them. The mother screamed as she saw her daughter lying in a pool of blood. One shot was fired that caught the mother in the middle of her forehead. She tumbled down the stairs as the frighten man stood motionless. "Dave Weston?" one man asked. Dave could only shake his head. The other man grabbed Dave off the staircase and pushed him to the couch. "We got a few questions for you." For twenty minutes they beat and asked Dave questions about his car how he got stuck up in the dope house and who owns the blue Toyota car in his name. Dave never answered. A bullet entered his leg and Dave screamed. As he screamed a five year old girl appeared on the staircase rubbing her eyes. "Daddy, Mommy" she said. The man close to the stairs shot. The bullet caught the little girl in her head a knocked her up in the air four feet. Her limp body slid back down the stairs. Dave could not believe his eyes he jumped for the man with the gun on him. He almost had it away from him when he felt the hot lead explode inside his head.

    I sat there looking at the phone for a minute trying to gather my thoughts. Something didn't feel right. I told Cye and she suggested I call the guys and they can follow me. I called Reggie and he said he and Whitey went on a mission and should be back by tomorrow. I knew they had to get that product working before it went bad. I called Perk and Jimmy and they said they would be ready in an hour. I went upstairs to take a shower. I heard Cye yelling my name and I came running down the stairs naked with my gun in my hand. "What's wrong?" I asked. "The news somebody killed Dave." She said. "Dave? I thought he got straight and went back to his family." "He did and his family got killed. Two little girls and a woman were killed. "Cye said while holding her mouth in disbelief. The news caster said they were shot execution style and it looked like Dave was tortured. This wasn't good for us. Did he talk? Did he tell them my real name? Did he tell them how we met? I called Reggie back and told him what happen. He said I should chill until he gets back in the morning. I told him if I didn't meet Dom he would think something is up. He told me don't go nowhere alone. Dom called me back and we set up a meet in a public place. We took Cye's car and had Perk follow us in the black car. Jimmy stayed at the house so he could keep an eye on the money. We left my car in case Jimmy needed to make a run. As soon as we left Jimmy decided to go get some cigarettes at the corner store. He pulled in the store and didn't notice the two white men asking the owner questions. He got his cigarettes and left. The two men who had left the store before him noticed the blue Toyota in the parking lot. When Jimmy came out they followed him. Jimmy started to park in the back of Cye and my house then he remembered he wanted a DVD to watch. So he pulled up in back of the guy's house. He got out went inside to retrieve the DVD. When he was leaving he opened the door and the two men pushed their way in with their guns out. Jimmy tried to reach for his gun and was shot on his side. The blood poured out as the other man surveyed the house to see if anyone else was inside. Jimmy fell to the ground in pain and doubled over. The other man followed his partner cautiously turning his back on Jimmy. Jimmy pulled the gun in his ankle hoister and begun firing. He hit one guy twice in the back before the second man peered from behind him and shot Jimmy three times in his chest. The first man fell down but he wasn't hurt because he had on a bullet proof vest. His partner helped him up and made sure he was alright.

The house was ransacked looking for drugs money. They found fifty thousand dollars that Reggie had and no drugs. They tore up all the furniture and clothes.

Cye and I met with Dom. I think he wanted me to come by myself but mama didn't raise no dummy. Cye had her guns inside her jacket pocket and I had one in my purse and the other in my back under my blouse. We approached Dom with caution and ours eyes open ready for battle if necessary. Dom was sitting on a park bench with a lot of kids playing around. Cye sat on one side of him and I on the other. Dom didn't look good. He looked like he hadn't been sleeping or either he was getting high. He looked worried. "What's wrong Dom? You look terrible." I said. "I hired you girls to protect me and now that you haven't been around so much somebody is trying to kill me." "Dom you don't know what you want. You want us to be your partner or you want us to watch your back. We can't do both." Cye said. "I know, but so much is going on" he said. "Well what's happening?" I asked. He put his head down and his eyes got watery. "Somebody killed my baby's mama" "The girl that set you up, I thought you didn't care" I said. "They almost killed my son. We were trying to work things out. I moved in with her for my son." He said. "So all the bull shit you been trying to run on me was a lie. You were just trying to get with me and when you got what you wanted you stepped back." I yelled turning the tables kicking him more while he was down. "You did what?" "I knew I should have killed that bitch when I had the chance." Cye said. "So what do you want from us" "My uncle think that you set me up to get robbed." Dom said. "How can I set you up stupid, I was with you. I was collecting your money." I said. "I know that's what I told my uncle. I just wanted to let you know to watch your back. My family is ruthless and sometimes I don't agree with their tactics." He said. "I still want you ladies to watch my back with no strings attached. We'll split all the profits. But you have to roll where I roll. Is that cool?" "I don't know Dom, I can't trust you,

you been lying to us. Plus we are only going to be her a month or so. Cye's dad is getting worse and when we leave we're not coming back. We have to watch her mother." I said. "Ok, But when they robbed me they took all my product and money. I will have to get 20 kilos from my uncle I just want to flip that. Please can we do that?" He asked. "Dom this shit is getting to confusing. You say your uncle thinks we set you up. Then you say you want us to go with you to get 20 k from your uncle. You think we stupid." Cye pulled her gun out of her jacket and stuck it in Dom's back. "I'm tired of being caught in the middle. "Sis, why don't we just do him here and leave?" Dom got nervous as I pandered the answer. Dom jumped up and turn toward Cye "I'm getting tired of you pulling guns on me you think I'm some punk" he said. A man appeared from behind the bench with his gun out pointing it at Cye's head. You alright Dominique he asked. Before I could draw my gun and Dom could answer the man was struck in the head with a gun butt. The kids started yelling and screaming. The parents were running scooping up their kids. Perk had his gun in the man's face. "Hold on wait. We are all family up here. I'm sorry Cye" Dom yelled. "Relax Perk everything is cool" I said. Perk put his gun down to his side and helped the man up. He just looked at him and didn't say a word. The man looked at Perk with revenge in his eyes. Cye put her gun up and just looked at me. She really wanted to blow Dom away. "We got to get out of hear the police will be here in a minute." I said. Everybody start walking away. Dom stopped me and said meet him at the house tomorrow at one o'clock. He kissed me on the cheek and asked "are we cool Keysha?" "I'm sorry Dom for not being sensitive to what you're going through. I guess I like you more then I think. I'll see you tomorrow." I said and walked away. Cye, Perk and I walked around the park first to make sure no one was following us. Cye and I got in her car and Perk followed in the cutlass. "Cye don't worry the right time will come. I know you wanted to dead Dom. But see we didn't even know he had backup and you would have got hurt before we could respond." I said "I know Tee, but I'm getting frustrated. I want to finish this so I can live my own life. Try to be happy" She said. "Cye we have to concentrate on the big picture. We want all their family. Just be patient girl." "Ok Tee I'm trying." The ride back we talked about happiness. We talked about what we wanted to be doing in the next five years. We talked about my daughter Carletha and how old she would be and about Cye's sister Judge Collins. I know she really missed her sister. We turned the music up and sung with Melanie Fiona. If you can't give it to me right, don't give it to me at all. Our mood had change and we were laughing and joking by the time we got to the house.

Chapter 14

They Killed Jimmy Somebody is Going To Pay

Cye and I went in the house and Perk parked the cutlass in the garage. He asked Cye if she felt like fixing something to eat. Cye said ok and to come back in an hour. She looked at Perk and said "Thanks Perk for having my back" "We all fam here. I will always have you guys back." He said as he disappeared in the house. Neither Cye nor I had our keys out so we both looked at each other and laughed. I reached in my purse. "The Fuck" is all we heard coming from Perk's house. "Hell naw" he yelled. Both Cye and I ran over to the guys house two doors down with our guns out. Perk was holding his boy Jimmy. They killed Jimmy. They killed my boy." He yelled. When we entered the house we saw Jimmy's body close to the back door. We carefully went inside holding our guns up like veteran police officer's. The house was torn up. Everything was broken. We searched the house in every corner before we returned to where Jimmy's body was. Perk was still holding him like he was expecting him to wake up. I pulled out my phone and called Reggie. When he answered I said. "Reggie Jimmy's dead." "What" he said "How" "Somebody killed him at the house while we were meeting Dom. They tore up the house and furniture looking for something. I Hope you didn't have anything there." I asked. "I left the money you gave me there, that's it Fifty thousand. Are you and Cye alright? How's Perk?" "Reggie he messed up man. He wants to go kill everybody at that house we were at. He said he just feels they got something to do with it. He saw the guy write down my license number." "Tee keep him at your house. I think these guys are smarter than we think. We got to move. But nobody leaves the house until we get there. Let me talk to Perk." I gave Perk the phone and heard him say ok over and over. Then he said I'm cool. Then he gave me the phone back. "I'll bring some recruits. Don't let anybody leave the house. Gather up all the essentials and tonight will be your last night there." I said ok and he asked to talk to Cye. Cye took the phone as we walked back to our house. Perk picked up Jimmy's guns took Jimmy's wallet and wiped down the house before he came down to our house.

    Cye went upstairs and took a shower. I stayed downstairs and talked to Perk. He was withdrawn. I asked him who he thought did it and why. His theory was Dom's uncle trying to see if we set him up. I found some cigarettes in Jimmy's pocket. So he must have went to the store to buy them because he didn't have any earlier. They must have noticed your car and followed him from the store. He asked me to tell him about Dave and what happened to him. Cye came back down and joined us. She had to remind me that I put the car in Dave's name. That might be how they tracked us so fast. She fixed a couple of sandwiches and we ate and drank wine. We told Perk everything. We told him about why we were in California and how we got to California. Cye told him about the deaths of her parents every detail. We told him about my mother being killed protecting my daughter. Perk told us about his past with Reggie. He and Jimmy was basically their enforcer for the last few years. We talked until late in the morning. Perk said that he was alright and we should go to bed. We gave him some cover and he asked me for some duck tape. When I got it for him I asked him what he needed it for. He said that he would protect us and if we heard shots come down shooting. He showed us how he wrapped the tape around his hand with the gun. He taped his trigger finger so that the gun wouldn't fall out of his hand if he fell asleep. I liked that. So I asked him to show me by doing my hand. He wrapped mine and I went to sleep with my gun. It was uncomfortable at first but soon I was sleep. I never had to sleep with a gun before but I wanted to make sure that I could if I had to.

It was 9:30 before we were waken by a heavy knock on the door. Perk jumped up gun pointing at the door half asleep. I guess this is the only downfall with having your gun taped to your hand. You can wake up and start shooting before you realize it. Reggie and Whitey came into the house followed by six other gentlemen. I heard them talking. Reggie said they had cleaned everything out of the house and wiped everything down with bleach. Packed all the clothes up and put them in the van. They made plans on the next move. Their plans were well thought out and put us out of California in two weeks. I cleaned up and came downstairs just as Cye was walking out her room. "Good morning, you all right?" I asked she looked a little pale. " I'm fine didn't sleep to well. Need to get me something to eat." She said as she headed straight for the kitchen not noticing the guys in the dining room. Reggie followed her in the kitchen and he came out smiling. I didn't pay too much attention about what was going on with them because Whitey was introducing me to the other guys. Two of them I knew from back in the day. They were Carl and Reggie's cousins. I knew by the looks on their faces somebody was going to pay for Jimmy's death. I looked at Cye and she had a look of content something I haven't seen on her face in years. We all sat down and talked about the plan of action. Reggie had a plan. We all listened. Reggie assumed his old roll of the top enforcer. He told all the eight guys that were present Cye and Teeka are our main concern. We must protect the ladies at all cost by any means necessary. Cye and I got dressed and we all left. Perk rode with Cye and me. Reggie and Whitey rode in their BMW. The six guys followed us keeping a block distance in the van. I had an appointment with Dom at the house. We rode to the drop house cautiously. Perk, Cye and I got out to enter the house. Perk pushed us back and made us wait until he saw that no one was inside. We went in to set up. My cell phone that was on vibrate rung twice. I knew Dom was on his way in. The two rings meant he had two guys with him. Perk stopped them at the door.

"Who the fuck you think you are going to search" Dom asked. Cye and I had our guns drawn. "Dom, everybody coming in this door here is getting searched. They killed one of my cousins and my family is very upset." I said. "I run this shit Kee not you. You can't search my people." He said. Perk and Cye had his two men against the wall. Perk turned around and hit Dom with his fist. Blood spattered out his nose. When one of the guys reached for his gun Cye shot him point blank. The bullet went through his neck as he fell to the ground. The other guy put his hands up in the air. Perk put his gun to Dom's temple. "You want to talk" I said "let's talk" "What's going down Kee you trying to take over my business?" he asked. "I don't want your business Dom. If I had wanted it I would have been took it from you. You brought two of you goons in her to talk to me. What you wanna talk about Dom? You want to talk about why you killed my cousin. If I had been driving my car you would have killed me too." I yelled. "Kee it's not like that. I didn't know they were going to kill your cousin. They were just making sure you didn't set me up and take my money." "So you had something to do with that?" "No that was my uncle, you know I wouldn't hurt you." He said. "But you would kill my cousin. Dom you have a problem." The man on the floor took his last breath. The second man pushed Cye hard and she fell to the floor. Perk and I turned around just to see the man bolt out the front door. We heard gun shots and then the door opened with the man holding his leg. Two men all dressed in black with scarfs over their face came in behind him. The AK assault rifles against his back. "Don't no body move. Everybody drop their guns." One of the masked men said. Perk went for his gun the assault rifle let off between four and ten shots. Everybody ducked for cover as Perk fell to the floor and didn't move. "What's going on Kee, Cece?" Dom asked. He was scared the words were stuttering out. "I'll give you money anything you want." Dom told the mask men. "I know you will give us what we want, but for now you call your uncle and your mama and tell them you have been kidnapped." The strong voice said. The assault rifles were no match for our weapons. So Cye and I pulled our guns out and threw them on the table. One of the mask men went to the back door and let in two more men. They also were dressed in black with scarf's and bullet proof vests. Tie them up he said pointing to Cye and me. The men tied us up and went over to Dom. "It's time for you to make that call." The man walked over to Dom pulled his cell phone from his case on his side and gave it to Dom. Dom dialed a number and spoke into the phone. "I have been kidnapped and I don't know what they want. Yes I'm at my drop house." The man took the phone from Dom. "We will be in contact and tell you what we want. Yes I know who the fuck I'm talking to. Chris Gucci. Now you wait for my call. We won't be here when you get here." The man hung up. He told his men to take Dom out the back door and wait. "We will leave them here for the Gucci family to find. "No, I yelled at them, they are going to kill us." Cye yelled untie us so we can leave. But the man just looked at us and left. One of Dom's men was dead and the other one was lying in a pool of blood. Cye was tied up and I was tied up. Perk was lying on the floor. He started to move. He begun to cough and he sat up pulled his shirt off and looked at his bullet proof vest. He untied Cye and I. He searched the other man again to make sure he wasn't armed. Then he went outside to his car. He returned with a gallon of gasoline. Perk pulled the dead man to the middle of the living room and he went over to the other man and helped him in the living room. Cye poured the gasoline on the dead man as the other man begin to plead. "Please don't, what you want?" he asked. "We only got a few minutes before your boss get here. Now I'm only going to ask one time. "How long have you been working for the Guccci's" The man said ten years. I told him I wanted the addresses of all the Gucci family members including parents. If he gave it to us we would leave now. I gave him one minute. Perk took the gas can from Cye and start pouring gasoline on the man's wound. He started yelling and screaming from

151

the burning on his leg. He gave in saying addresses and streets. Hoping the pain would stop. He even told us who lived at each address. Cye wrote everything down he said. Fifteen minutes had passed and we had to leave before reinforcements came. Perk took his gun out and shot the man in the head twice, saying this is for Jimmy. Cye and I ran outside to the car and noticed Reggie and Whitey standing guard. Perk threw his cigarette at the man watched as the flames started. He slammed the door and jumped in the car. We drove off and Reggie and Whitey followed in their car. Cye looked at the addresses that was on the paper.

Chapter 15   Another Gucci Dies

On the other side of town the guys in the van pulled up to a warehouse. They pushed a button on the remote and the large door opened. Dom could hear the sound of the door chains cranking up. He feared for his life. The van stopped and Dom heard footsteps as the door opened. The guys pulled him out the van and put him in a chair that already had handcuffs on it. It was cuffed to an iron pipe coming out of the wall. The men cuffed Dom and told him to sit and don't make a sound. The men put a blind fold over Dom's eyes as he started screaming. One blow to Dom's head silenced him as he fell unconscious. A cell phone rang and one of the guys answered and said ok. Three of the guys jumped in the truck opened the door and left. The guy left closed the door and told Dom to be quiet. At the home of Chris Gucci two men knocked on the door. Just as Sarkis and Hal, Chris Gucci's hired killers with a badge, reached the drop house. They saw fire trucks and a lot of police vehicles. They took their badges out and approached the house. A couple of the police officer's spoke and another one asked "Sarkis what you doing here I thought you were on a case." "Me and Hal was going to a see an informant when we heard the call. Just want to see what happen then we are out of here." Sarkis said. "Alright, let them in." The house fire was in one room. In that room two charcoaled bodies laid in the middle of the floor. "You guys ID them yet" Hal asked. "Not yet we can't tell if they are white or black" one of the policemen said. Hal and Sarkis left and went to call Chris Gucci. They didn't know if one of the dead bodies was Dom their bosses' nephew. The phone kept ringing and ringing. Back at Chris Gucci's house the two men entered with their badges around their neck. They were let in by the bodyguard. Then they were taken to the den to see Chris. Chris was at his desk and had his back to the two men. "I'm not paying another one of you guys. I got four badge totting killers and my nephew still gets kidnapped." "We have a little news about your nephew" Whitey said. Chris turned around in his chair. Just when he looked up Reggie put two bullets in his bodyguard one in his chest and one in his forehead. The guns had silencers on them so all you heard was a thump. Whitey pulled his gun as Chris Gucci watched his bodyguard fall to the floor. He got focused when Whitey smacked him in the face with his gun. Blood came out of his nose and he tried to go in his desk to get a hanky. His hand touched his gun as he pulled it out of the desk drawer. He felt a hot sting in his shoulder which caused him to drop the gun to the floor. Reggie said "Next one is for keeps. Who else is in the house?" he asked. Chris started to say no one but Whitey's gun caught him again across the top of his head. Chris screamed in pain. "Who else is in the house?" Whitney asked. Blood streaming from his head and his face Chris said between blooded lips. "My wife and daughter are up stairs please don't hurt them what is this about?" he screamed. Whitey went upstairs and got the woman and the girl who was about eighteen years old. They came down screaming Whitey hit the lady "Shut the fuck up" he said. Chris was begging "What is this about? I got money, you want money?" he begged. "I'm not going to tell you again. Everybody shut up." Reggie said. "Please just tell me what this is about?" Chris said in a mild voice. Whitey walked up to Chris like they had rehearsed this. "About a year ago three people were killed at a beach house in Fresno California. They had large sums of money and drugs in the house. Somebody took my five million dollars. Your brother Mark got knocked for the job so I figure you must have my money." Whitey said. Chris took the bait like a baby taking his bottle. He thought that he could save his family by telling the truth. "There was no money in that house" he said before he realized that he was snitching. Reggie and Whitey looked at each other as Whitey kept probing the questions. "We had 10 kilo's in there and five million. You are trying to tell me that nothing was there even though I dropped the money off myself that morning at nine o'clock." Whitey turned around and shot the woman in the chest. Chris tried to get up but Reggie hit him with the butt on the gun. "Where is the money" he asked. Chris screamed in terror watching his wife's eyes fade off to the other side of life. "There was no money. We went in the house looking for the girl that killed my brothers. They wouldn't talk so we killed the rest of the family. Reggie shot Chris in his other shoulder. He grimaced in pain. Whitey walked over to the front door peeked out the window. He waved to Perk who was standing on the porch with his gun to his side to come in. The door opened and we came in. Perk, Cye and myself. The look on Chris's face told the story. He knew who I was. His daughter kneeling over her mother's lifeless body looked up and saw the look on her father's face. Fear begun to take its toll and she cried mercifully. Chris looked into my eyes as I looked in his. I pulled my gun and walked over to the daughter.

"Get up" I said. I pushed her to where Chris was sitting. I grabbed her hair and banged her head on the desk. Then I put my gun to the back of her head. I cocked the gun to put a bullet in the chamber. "I want to know exactly what happen on my families last day. Don't leave anything out because if you do I'll kill your daughter right here." I said. Chris Gucci started ratting like he had some cheese waiting on him. He told us every little detail. I didn't even notice Cye walk over to my side. She held my hand and cried. When I turned toward her to give her a hug she pulled the gun out with her other hand shot the girl four times. Blood splattered all over me and her. She looked like she was in a trance. Reggie cocked his gun and asked Chris. "Who else was with you?" "It was the two policeman Sarkis and Hal." Chris said. "Why did your brother Mark get locked up on that case?" I asked. "He is only going to do three years. Somebody had to take the fall." "Who killed my cousin yesterday" Reggie asked. "The same two guys" Chris started crying and screaming looking at the dead girl in front of him. "I told my brother I'd watch out for his daughter and you killed her." That brought some sort of closer to Cye she wiped away the tears and pulled the trigger again. The bullet hit Chris in the head. It caught all of us by surprise. I turned and emptied my gun in Chris's body. Perk was at the front door. He opened it and went outside to see if everything was cool. We all walked out and got in our cars. As we drove down the big driveway I saw the van on the outside of the gate with four heavy armed guys in it. I thought to myself it is good to have family that has your back.

Sarkis and Hal made their way back to Chris Gucci's house. They had called Chris numerous times and also called the body guard watching him. They didn't get an answer from either. Their suspicious were getting to them. As police officer's they had a gut feeling something was wrong. They pulled up the driveway and everything was quiet. They drew their guns and approached the house. They tried to open the door but it was locked. They decided to call for back up and kicked the door in. The sight of the three bodies lying there brought a tear to Sarkis eyes. He had grown up with the Gucci's and also promised Mark that he would look after his daughter. To see her lying there in a pool of blood with bullet holes in her head caught him off guard. Police were everywhere in three minutes. A sergeant came in and asked Sarkis and Hal if they knew who was responsible for these gruesome murders. Hal said he didn't know but he knew the victim's nephew had been kidnapped. That's why they came by to talk to Chris. The sergeant assigned them to the case. So we now had the California police force looking for us and two rouge cops. Sarkis and Hal got more upset when they thought about not being able to get the twenty five thousand a month they had been receiving from the Gucci family for protection. Ahead of them were a lot of sleepless nights following this case.

Mama Raised A Killer II

Chapter 16

Dom Kidnapped But Finds An Ally

At the vacant warehouse Dom asked the man watching him for a cigarette. The man gave him a lighted cigarette. Dom asked the man questions but he never answered. He asked him had he ever had a million dollars. The man responded no. Dom then told him he could get to a million dollars in thirty minutes and he could be in the Bahamas's by night fall. The man listened. He had thought about getting out the game. To have a million to his self meant no more taking orders. "We could be back at my house in a few minutes I got two million there you can take one." Dom pleaded. "I'll take the other and we will never see each other again." "You want me to cross my family" the man asked. "Have your family ever giving you that much money? What's your name?" Don asked.

The man was silent for a minute before he said TJ. "So you want me to let you go and my family will kill me." TJ said. "No Dom said. We leave together my family is the connection on the west coast. We will protect you and get you out the country." "I can't spend any money if I'm dead." TJ said. Dom's mind was spinning. He knew he might die. He was trying to bargain a way to stay alive. "Are you with the Mexican's" Dom asked. TJ didn't answer. "I tell you what, TJ or whatever your name is. I'm going to trust you and tell you where the money is. Shit I can't spend it if I'm dead like you said. You feel me?" Dom asked. TJ shook his head letting him know he was listening. "I'm going to have to trust in you. Trust that if you have an opportunity after you get the money, you will let me go. Is that fair?" TJ just looked at Dom strangely. Dom asked him for a pen. Dom reached in his pocket with his free hand and got a card out. He wrote directions on it and explained to TJ what to do. TJ didn't have a response. He had to think about it. Crossing

Reggie and the crew he will come up dead. But for a million he could get lost in another country. TJ took the card looked Dom in his eyes and said. "I will think about it." "That's all I can ask that you think about it. When you get the money you will see I'm serious." Dom said. The door to the warehouse opened up and three guys came in. Still in all black with scarfs on half their face the same as TJ. "The Boss giving you a brake we are going to watch him for a while." One guy left and TJ followed and the door closed behind them.

Outside the warehouse Reggie, Whitey, Perk, Cye and I were waiting. There were four guys in the van including TJ. Cye looked at the addresses on the paper. The one that caught her eyes was Dom's mother. She knew Dom's child would properly be there. As they drove to the new address TJ's mind was on the money. How could he pull this off without getting dead? He thought about taking a partner but who could he trust. Two of the crew is Reggie's cousins. TJ looked around the van at the other three men. No one was looking at him. He stuck his finger deep down his throat. He gagged and threw up the little food he had that day. The driver stopped the van and TJ threw up as soon as the door opened. The guys in the cars ahead pulled over. The driver's cell phone rang. It was Reggie "What's wrong" he yelled in the phone. "TJ is sick" the driver said. "Is he all right? We can't stop in the middle on the street with this much arsenal." Reggie said. The driver asked TJ if he was alright. He said he must have ate some bad food. He told the driver he will take a cab to the hotel and wait until they called him. He told Reggie what he said and Reggie said Ok. They pulled off as you could see TJ doubled over throwing up. He stayed bent over and gagging until the cars were out of sight. TJ had one thing on his mind money. The talk with Dom was beginning to take his toll on his thought process. To have a million dollars was all he thought about. He didn't think about the consequences when he got the money. TJ looked around to make sure no one was looking then he straighten himself up and went looking for a cab.

Sarkis and Hal went back to the precinct to try to get a lead on the murders at Chris Gucci's house. They decided to follow the Gucci family's past. While checking their intelligence they saw that two of the Gucci brothers were killed in Detroit. John and George migrated to Detroit from California to set up their own drug empire. They learn that George Gucci was killed by jumping out of a window at his doctor's office. The killing was ruled questionable. The file said that the doctor said he had worked on a drug dealer at gun point a couple of weeks before. They couldn't find his secretary to verify. John Gucci's file showed he had gotten killed on a downtown Detroit Street. The detective thought it was a revenge gone bad. His body was filled with bullets and a drug dealer was found dead right next to John Gucci. The file said the man was killed by John Gucci's gun. The drug dealer was believed to be the same man that the doctor worked on but the doctor would not identify him. He feared for his family's safety. There was a young woman tried for the murder but later beat the case. There was no file or pictures of the woman. Her attorney must have had all the files expunged. "Hal" Sarkis said "We have to fly to Detroit to get more information on this case. I got a feeling these murders might tie into the Chris Gucci's death." Hal looked at Sarkis and got up and headed straight for the door. The two policemen were on the next plane out of California heading for Detroit. The two policemen arrived at Metro Detroit Airport in three and a half hours. They had a police sergeant waiting on them. It was the arresting officer on the John Gucci murder. He told them about the case and the girl who got off on the murder. Internal affairs suspected connection of corruption in the justice system. His theory was that someone was paid to get the girl off. As the detective kept talking, Sarkis remembered that Chris Gucci had him look for a girl he had thought killed his brothers. But she was in California. Chris and his brother Mark had killed a family and Mark is doing a short bit for it. Sarkis looked at this partner with a devilish grin. "What's up?" asked Hal. Both the detective and Hal waited for an answer. "Detective can you please copy these file's for me and my partner. We have all the information we need. Thank You." Sarkis and Hal went outside to smoke a cigarette. Sarkis told Hal about his thoughts and he said that the Detroit killers where connected to the California killings. "We got all we need here we have to get back to California." The two men went back inside the precinct. The detective brought the copy of the file. Hal asked him if he could drop them back off at the airport.

Chapter 17

TJ Turns On His Crew

Teeka looked at the addresses on the piece of paper. "Where we going next" Cye asked. The four addresses each had names of a Gucci family member. I took a moment to think. We had to work this plan perfect. If we didn't hit each house at the right time the others will be notified. Then the element of surprise will no longer be in our favor. We decided to hit Mike Gucci's house. He is the last brother out of the five. He would be the easiest one because he was a lawyer and not directly in the game. He handled all the legal matters for the family. He lived in Beverly Hills California. It took us about an hour before we started seeing all the beautiful homes and mansions. Whitey had a GPS and we followed the black BMW him and Reggie where driving in. I was with

Cye and Perk in Cye's car. The black van with the heavily armed men, were trailing us by a block. We came up on the block looking for the address when Reggie called my cell phone. "It is not the right time" he said. "What you mean what's wrong?" I asked. "Look around it must be a hundred cars on this block and the last one. People are over here paying their respect." He said. "Oh yea, they did lose a few relatives in the last couple of days." "We have to be patient our time will come." He said. "What you want to do" I asked. "Whitey had an ideal. We going to stop and get something to eat before we get back to LA." He said. "Let me talk to Whitey?" I asked. Whitey got on the phone. He asked me if I was alright. Then he said he could still smell my scent on his body. We both laughed. He then told me he went to school at UCLA and he could get a lead on where Mike Gucci's office was. He said he needed a day or so. I said that was cool. "Teeka I just want to hold you and talk like we did the other night. I really enjoyed your company." Whitey said. "I'd like that Whitey we will follow you back" I said then hung up the phone. The car was silent but I could feel Cye looking at me wanting to ask me something. Or either tease me but Perk was in the car so I escaped that one. We drove for about twenty minutes. Then we pulled up to a nice restaurant off the highway. Reggie and Whitey got out of their car and approached ours. They told us to come on in we could sit down and talk. Perk said he was going with the guys in the van. They went to the Mc Donalds next to the restaurant. We went it and were seated in the back. The place was an Italian restaurant and reminded me of one of those restaurants in the movies about Al Capone. It was a nice family restaurant. We sat a booth and Reggie sat next to Cye and Whitey sat next to me smiling. "What you smiling for?" I asked. "I have been waiting on this moment for a while" he said. Cye and Reggie just laughed. I just look deep in Whitey's eyes. I could see softness and gentleness. I seem to looking at the inside of his heart. But I knew on the outside he was a natural killer. My mind was deep in thought looking in his eyes as he was still looking in mine. The waitress came over and asked if we would like something to drink. To my surprise everybody ordered water. We all thought alike. We knew we had to keep our mind focus. When the waitress came back we ordered food. We sat and talked and just enjoyed our lunch. We didn't talk any business. Whitey got up to call some guys he went to school with to see if he could get a lead on Mike Gucci. My cell phone startled me since I didn't think it would ring I was with everybody close to me. I looked at the caller ID it was Perk. "Hello" I answered. "Tee four guys pulled up in a Hummer one of them looked just like Dom. Before I did something one of the guys in the van called the garage. Dom is still tied up. What you want me to do?" he asked. "Stay on point" I said and hung up. I told Cye and Reggie as the men entered the restaurant. They went and sat at the bar and two others sat by the door. The young guy did look like Dom. But he was flashier he looked like a drug dealer. Lots of jewelry new clothes and gym shoes he acted like he was in control. Cye looked at me "Who is that? You think they came here for us?" she asked. "Cye how they know where or who we are? He probably doesn't know anything about us." We could see them from where we were seated, but they couldn't see us. I could tell this wasn't Dom. This guy was loud and mouthy. Reggie took out his cell phone and called Whitey who was still in the rest room on the phone. We were through eating and ready to leave. Everybody had their hand on their guns. I put one in my chamber after unlocking it. We got up ready to face our destiny. "Wait a minute" Reggie said. You ladies wait here until after we leave. Perk and the guys in the van will make sure you make it back to LA. He didn't wait for an answer he got up to head toward the rest room. Whitey was already out and walking toward the men. I pulled my gun out and put it under the table. Cye did the same. Before he could reach the guy that looked like Dom the two guys at the door were up in front of him. "Dom" Whitey said. Dom you not going to holla at your boy?" The guy turned around as the two guys stopped Whitey from reaching the young man. "Oh, It's like this Dom?" Whitey said. "Look my man I'm not Dom?" "Oh now you don't know me after I hooked you up with them fine sisters in LA." Whitey said, sounding so convincing. "Let him go" the young man said to his bodyguards. Whitey sat down on the seat next to him. "Look dude let me buy you a drink, I'm not Dom I'm his cousin JJ John Jr" he said. "For real man you two look like twins man." Whitey said. "Our fathers were twins." "Man that's deep" Whitey said as he watched Reggie pass him and go outside. That was his cue to leave. "Man I'll take a rain check on that drink. Tell Dom Tyrone said get at me" Whitey said as he got up and extended his hand to the young man. They gave each other the brothers hand shake. It looked funny for two white looking guys giving each other dap. "Be cool" the young man said as Whitey walked out the door. After ten minutes the young man and his crew got up and left. Cye and I put our guns back in our purses and left a few minutes later. Whitey and Reggie were gone following the Hummer. Perk was posted outside the door of the restaurant waiting on us. We got in Cye's car and drove back to LA with the van following a block behind.

TJ had the cab driver take him to the storage complex. He got out and told the cab driver to wait. He then entered the code on the card at the gate. He then proceeded to storage B-41. He opened the lock with the combination written of the card. When he opened the door he saw a small arsenal and a jewelry box. He looked into the box and was at awe of all the watches and bracelets. TJ then decided he will kill Dom and take everything in the storage. TJ went to the back and looked in a cardboard box. There he discovered two duffle bags. In the bags was money. Lot's of money. TJ never saw so much money. He sat there and counted as high as he could. He stopped at $100,000. He looked at his watch and knew he had to get back before his shift to guard Dom. TJ grabbed the two duffle bags and a hand full of jewelry on his way out. He got back in the cab and drove back to where to warehouse was. He had the cab driver stop at a expensive hotel. He gave him a hundred dollars and said he would give him another if he waited. TJ went in and registered in the Hilton Hotel took his bags to the room and put the Do Not Disturb sign on the door. TJ had the cab driver drop him at the warehouse.

TJ knocked on the gate of the warehouse. The two men guarding Dom jumped. They knew anyone coming in could open the door from the outside. But you had to have a key to slide the chains. They could open it from the inside but were told not to. They looked at each other. "Something could have gone wrong, we better see who it is." One of the guys said. "You open it and I'll watch Dom and the door. If it is some of his people I'll kill him first." He said. "Alright open the door." The door was opened slowly and TJ stood there without his scarf on. "What the fuck are you doing here man?" The man at the door asked. "I got sick and they dropped me off so I'm here to take over my shift." TJ said. "Give me your scarf and gear then you can take a break until the van comes." "Cool man I'm starving" The man couldn't wait to take his gear off. He handed the man his scarf, vest and weapon then went out the door. TJ closed the gate and walked to the back of the warehouse. The man watching Dom was still a little suspicious. He held his gun to Dom's head as TJ walked toward them. Dom eyes got big even though he was fading in and out from lack of food. "Give him some water man. Can't you see he aint going to make it. Then Reggie is going to be all in your ass." TJ said. The man looked at him "I don't take any orders from you. You want him to have some water you get it." The man said. TJ went and got Dom some water out the bathroom. He held it while Dom drank it. Looking straight in Dom's eyes he winked. Dom got a little energy from the water and the thought that he might go free. TJ turned around as the man guarding Dom was walking away. He shot him in his back. The bullet spun him around and TJ shot him again. He stumbled to the floor. TJ went over to Dom took off his scarf and said. "I got the money you didn't tell me about the jewelry." "You can have the jewelry and anything else you want." Dom said. TJ's head was spinning dollar signs. He never had any money of his own. He wanted to buy a house and some horses and a farm. He wanted to move to the country and get away from the city. Now he had the opportunity to fulfill his dreams. He has happy and the fear went away when he thought about the money. "Un tie me" Dom yelled. TJ thought about killing Dom right there but that would have everybody looking for him since the other guy left knows I was here. He decided that he would kill Dom when they got some where safe. He untied Dom. Dom ran to the restroom. He had been holding his urine because he didn't want to look like a punk peeing on himself. He peed and threw some water on his face. He thought for a minute how he was going to get the money away from TJ. Dom had a secret part in the bags that held guns in them. If he could get to the money he knew he could surprise TJ and kill him. When Dom came out the bathroom he asked TJ "where is the money" "It's in the Hilton up the street" "You get my million too." He asked. "Yes I got it. We need to get out of here before the other guys come back. TJ walked to the gate and pulled the chains to open the door. Dom was in the doorway anxious to get outside. He hadn't seen daylight or freedom in a couple of days. All he thought about was his son. He had decided when he was tied up that if he got out of this alive he was going to get out the game and move over seas with his son. The door opened and the sun light hit Dom in his face. He couldn't adjust his eyes to the sunlight. As he walked out with TJ behind him he heard two gunshots. Dom felt a sharp pain in his arm. He reached over with his other hand to feel the blood coming out. TJ was shot in his shoulder. The automatic weapon dropped to the ground. TJ looked up to see the van and the other four guys with their guns on him. "What you doing man? You turn on your family for a white man." One guy said. "Let me kill him" another one said. Perk said everybody inside. Dom was pushed inside and TJ was being kicked inside. His loyal partners had no mercy on him. The guys walked to the back as Perk motioned for Cye and I to come in before he closed the gate. I called Reggie and he said he and Whitey was five minutes away. "Why you do it TJ?" one of the guys asked. TJ looked at them and said he gave me a million dollars. I never had no money guys I'm sorry. What would you do?" "I wouldn't cross my family." The man shot him. TJ still in pain yelled "I'm sorry" "Where is the money, he promised you money you haven't seen TJ?" he asked. "I got the money it's at the hotel with a lot of jewelry. I was going to kill him and split it with you guys." "You killed my cousin, he laying here dead and you alive it ain't fare" another man said. He shot TJ in his hand. TJ screamed "The money is in the Hilton room 406 you can go get it. There is two million in there we all can have a piece." One of the other guys walked up to TJ didn't speak he shot him in his leg. This was a ritual I had seen before. Carl and Reggie's crew believe in loyalty. Perk had done this before and he stayed in front of us with his gun out. Dom was tied up again and grimmest with every shot. Tears were running down his face. The blood flowing from his body was weakening Dom. The last two men shot TJ with both of them shooting him in his head. The gate to the warehouse opened it was Reggie and Whitey. They looked at Cye and me and asked "You guys aright." We are fine" Cye said. She walked over to Reggie and pulled him to the door and they talked for a couple of minutes. I thought she was filling Reggie in on what happened. The next thing I know Cye came to me and said she will be right back. She called Perk and they left. Reggie pulled the gate down. I didn't ask any questions. I looked at Whitey and he was in his don't fuck with me mood. I was beginning to think that he didn't like seeing me caught up in all this drama. He wanted it to end and so did I. He nodded at me and went straight in the room. Dom looked up and saw Whitey and thought he was being rescued. His thoughts faded when Whitey asked the guys what happened and to take them dam scarf's off. Reggie walked to the back of the warehouse and joined the others. I knew right away that Dom was going to die in this warehouse. He would never be able to leave since he saw everybody's face. The guys were off to the side talking to Reggie and Whitey filling them in on what happened. The gate opened up after about twenty minutes. Cye and Perk came back in and closed the gate. Reggie told the guys to put the dead guys in the bathroom. Whitey told the guys "come on we are going to get that money." Dom yelled "That's my money" Cye walked from the back room as the guys were leaving. "You are not going to need it." Dom was puzzled. He knew that they all got ambushed together. When he saw me walk up with my gun out he just shook his head. The guys all left and the door was closed. Nobody was in the warehouse but us three. Perk was on the outside looking out.

"Keysha what's this about? You know I'm falling in love with you. I would never do anything to hurt you." Dom said. "I didn't set you up I was always real with you I really do care about you girls." I laughed "Do you think I could really fall in love with you?" I laughed again. I looked at Cye and she was looking so serious not a smile on her face. "Do you know who I am Dom?" "Yes you're Kee, what's this about?" "Dom I am the woman that killed your uncle" "What? My uncle" Dom said. "I killed your uncle John and I made George jump out a window before I killed him" "So what does that got to do with me" he asked. "You was born in the wrong family. You see your Daddy and your uncle Chris and those policemen your family pays killed my mother and Cye's mother and father." Cye eyes got watery and the tears started flowing. "Fuck this Tee, I let this mother fucker have sex with me knowing his family killed my parents. Now I want it back." "You want what back" Dom asked. Cye shot Dom in his leg. "Stand up mother fucker, stand up" Cye yelled. I put my gun to Dom's head as he tried to stand up. His hands were tied in front of him. I looked at Cye I didn't know what she about to do. "Pull your pants and underwear down." She said. Dom yelled "No Cece I'm sorry about your parents. But I didn't do it, please don't do this to me." Dom pleaded. "You did it to me didn't you." Cye shot Dom in his foot. Dom screamed in agony. I hit him with my gun butt. "Pull your pants off before I drop you right here." I said. Dom pulled his pants down and Cye pulled a bag out of her purse. She had a big meat cleaver in the bag and a pair of gloves. She slowly put the gloves on and said "Your Daddy raped my mother and made my father watch. Then he killed both of them. He them killed my aunt Tee's mother and tried to kill her child. After all that I laid down and fucked you. I want it back." "What back" Dom said. Cye didn't even reach down with one swipe she cut off his dick and his nuts. Part of his leg was open. Her cut was so swift and fast that the blood didn't come out right away. Cye held his blooded dick in her hand. She pulled out a pickle jar from her purse. She threw his genitals in the jar and screwed the top on. "I'm going to send this to your Daddy to see if he likes pickles. Dom fell to the floor screaming in pain. Holding his hand where his nuts use to be. Blood started gushing out his body like water. He screamed and moaned until he took his last breath. Cye stood over him and shot him once in the head and I shot him two more times. We hugged each other and cried for a few minutes. I spit on his dead body and Cye did also. We walked to the gate holding each other tight tears pouring out. We never had the time to mourn the death of our family. To us this was our way. We won't stop until we finish our mission of revenging our family.

Mama Raised A Killer II

Chapter 18

Getting What I Really Needed

Reggie and Whitey entered the Hotel looking suspiciously around. They took the elevator to the fourth floor. Reggie kept his hand on his nine millimeter automatic. He didn't know what to expect. Dom could have already called his people. They looked at the room numbers until they found 406. Both guys took their guns out while looking around for trouble. Whitey opened the door and they crept in with their guns ready to attack. They searched the room only found the two duffle bags. After looking in the bags they counted the money. They also found the jewelry and two pearl handle guns. Reggie looked at Whitey "We have two million dollars and another hundred thousand in jewelry." He said. "It's scary how we finding all this money. Dom had so much money he didn't know what to do with it."

Whitey said. "I think he was hiding money from his family not trying to let them know how big he was." Reggie said. The men sat back to think about what to do with the money. They had been having money fall in their lap since they got there. "Whitey we have to get out of here. Somebody is going to be looking for the money and the killer's." Reggie said. "Ok, we need to make a plan to get out of here in two weeks. I'm going to laundry some of this money through our off shore accounts." Whitey said. "We are going to give each guy $125,000 each. That way we can prevent them from crossing us for money. Reggie counted five bundles of $110,000 and four piles of $350,000 each. Whitey kept $50,000 for expenses. When they came outside everybody was waiting the four guys in the van Cye, Perk and me. Reggie and Whitey walked over to us and explained his plan. It was warm outside and we just sat on top on the guys and talked. It has been two days since Dom was kidnapped and I suggested that we hit all the houses to make sure we got all his money. Reggie was against it. Whitey was also. He said we have got enough money. People who get greedy get caught. I was stern with my decision. Cye was impartial she wouldn't give an answer but let it be known she was with me. We actually took a vote three guys said we should keep focus on our mission. The other two agreed with me. I folded my hand and said we let that slide and take a couple of days to set up a plan and a getaway plan. We really couldn't do anything until after the funerals. Unless you want to kill everybody at one time at the funeral, which I don't think is a good idea, too many witnesses. We decided to go to Santa Monica to stay in a hotel. Everybody had their own rooms. Reggie and Whitey had given everybody a stack of money. Everybody's mood was upbeat even with all the drama going on. Reggie and Cye got a suite and I had a connecting suite. I knew in my heart that Whitey would end up in my room but I let him wait a minute. Only a minute though, he really excited me. All the guys went shopping and to the tity bar. Whitey and I was in Reggie and Cye's room just chilling and talking. Whitey said. "I got something to tell you guys. My friend called and told me where Mike Gucci's office is. The guy that looked like Dom was John Jr. John Gucci's son. He runs a drug ring in Englewood. That's all the business we talking tonight, is that cool with you guys. I just want to relax and watch some TV." "Let's go get some movies" Cye said. We left to get some food and some movies. I ask Whitey if he was going to watch them with me. He looked at me like I was crazy. "I can't do that, I might fall asleep" he said. "So what's wrong with that" I asked. He just smiled and said ok. He grabbed my hand as we walked through Wal-Mart looking for movies. His touch made me feel so alive. I was blushing all over as he kept making me laugh. He was really a silly man. Cye saw that I was actually letting myself have fun. She looked at me and gave her approval as only close friends can. We went to a restaurant but we got a carry out. Cye and Reggie were kissing and hugging like they haven't seen each other in months. I can't really blame them we all haven't slept much in a couple of days. "Dam Cye, get a room" I said giving Cye a jealous look. She just looked at me a laughed. We got our food and drove back top t he hotel. Cye and Reggie disappeared in their room leaving Whitey and myself standing in the hallway. "Well are you going to watch a movie with me? I asked Whitey." "Yes I want to but I need to take a shower first." He said. "You can take a shower in my room" I said not knowing where that came from. He just smiled and said he had to go get something from his room. Ten minutes later Whitey knocked on the door. When he came in he had on some shorts and a wife beater tee shirt. I had never looked at is body because he always had on big clothes or a jacket to hide his gun. This man was looking good I stood there looking at his features and I could notice the black blood in his face. He had a thin nose and straight hair but his lips were fuller than a white man and the dimple made me blush. "Are you going to let me in or are you going to just stare at me." He asked. "I'm sorry" I said as I let him in checking out his butt that was also made like a black man. "I'm going to take a shower I'll be out in a minute as he disappeared in the bathroom and closed the door. I just stood there letting my thoughts consume me. The lust in my body was pouring out. The pent up anxiety of sexual desire was about to burst out of me. I almost came just thinking about his body and anticipating him making love to me. As my body burned with passion I walked to the bathroom hoping he didn't lock the door. I turned the door knob slowly. I didn't want to make any noise in case he wanted his privacy. The door knob slowly turned I thought it would stop half way if the door was locked. It kept turning until the door opened. I pushed the door slowly open and saw the shadow of Whitey through the glass shower doors. I stood there taking my clothes off piece by piece building up excitement watching this man rub his body down with soap. When I pulled my panties down they were sticking to my leg. They were wet I guess I came a couple of times. I walked in and opened the glass shower door. Whitey looked at me with his sexiest smile "I been waiting on you" he said. He helped me in the shower and pulled me under the water. He kissed my lips for the first time and my body and my heart immediate became his. I don't know if this was love at first kiss, lust, destiny or god. But at that moment I knew I would be all his. The water running through my hair and his hot tongue in my mouth excited me more. He stopped kissing and soaped up his wash cloth. He started washing me up. He washed my chest, arms, stomach and legs. He took his time on each part of my body. He was very gentle when he told me to open my legs as he washed my hot pussy. The water running down my back and his hands touching my body was pleasure I never felt before. He told me to turn around. He then washed my neck, back, ass, and my legs. He pushed me gently under the water to wash off. My hands were on the wall under the shower faucets enjoying the water run down my body. Then I felt Whiteys hot tongue on my back. He licked my neck and his tongue toured all parts of my back. I couldn't take it I came again before his hot tongue licked the inside line of my ass. He kept licking up and down on that line that god made to separate our butt cheeks. Dam that felt good. The next time his tongue when down the mason Dixon line it touched my wet moist pussy. I put my leg on the outside of the tub so he could reach my gold mine. His tongue found the wet spot. I think he couldn't take the anticipation any more. He replaced his tongue with a hard dick. It entered me slowly but the wetness let it go deeper and deeper. He stayed there bumping in and out of me for about five minutes. I came two more times. He turned me around and turned the water off the shower. He lifted me up and inserted his manhood inside of me again. I screamed in ecstasy as he was able to go all the way inside of my hot pussy. I pulled him closer to me holding on like my life depended on it. He pushed me against the shower wall and started sucking on my breast as he stroked slowly again and again inside my now vibrating body. I yelled his name "Whitey" as

I shook uncontrollably. He continued his assault on my wanting body. He kissed me again and I felt his juices spurt from his hard dick inside me. I again came and my fingers scratched his back. I tried to hold on to something while releasing the last bit of bent up tension I been holding on for years. I dug my fingers deep in his back and begin to cry. He put me down then asked me if I was all right. I just held on to him and he held me tight as the tears just poured out.

    We didn't watch movies that night. When we got out of the shower we just got in the bed and feel asleep in each other's arms. I woke up just as daylight was creeping in. I looked at Whitey laid on his stomach sleeping hard. I looked at all the scratches on his back and felt a little guilty. I say a little guilty because I enjoyed every minute that we shared in that shower. I pulled the sheet back and exposed his entire body. He was still sleep when I started kissing all the scratches on his back. He moaned every time my wet lips touched his back. I sat on his butt and begin kissing his neck. He moaned his approval as my tongue moved to his ear lops. When I stuck my wet tongue in his ear he jerked. I ran my hands through his straight hair and again kissed his neck. My tongue moved to his other ear. He jerked again when my tongue licked the insides of his ear. I made a mental note that he likes his ears licked. I continue licking his back and moved down. I took the same route he did and licked between his butt cheeks. I moved down and pried his legs about. I ran my tongue down his butt to his balls. I sucked his balls as he manhood started to rise. I licked up and down between his balls as his ass hole. He moaned and said dam baby. That turned me on more. I enjoyed seeing him in ecstasy enjoying what I was doing to him. He couldn't take any more so he turned over. His dick was hard. I got on top of it and slowly took what I could until I was able to sit all the way down on it. He pulled me forward so he could suck on my tities. I straighten my legs out and rode him while his hot tongue went for breast to breast. I came in a few minutes. I got up and turned around and sat on him. I moved up and down slowly. I begin to move side to side while going up and down. He was moaning and calling my name. I started moving faster when he grabbed my ankles. "Get this pussy, Whitey" I yelled over and over. He was banging away. Harder and harder the more I talked to him. I moved up and down flexing my muscles inside my stomach. He was saying softly, dam dam until he released himself from the torture of loving I was putting on him. I stayed on top of him and kept moving until I saw his toes curl up. I got off of him and put my head on his shoulders. His heart was beating so hard. We put in a movie and watched the movie each deep in our own thoughts. We drifted off into the afterglow of love making serenity. The movie watched us until I heard a knock on the adjoining suite door. I got up and let Cye in. She said that Reggie wanted a meeting with us in the parking lot around four o'clock.

"What time is it?" I asked. "It's after two, I see a glow in your eyes." She said. "Whitey must have hit that gee spot" I smiled and held my head down. Cye just laughed and said "Meet us down stairs at four. Make sure you bring Whitey" she closed the door laughing.

Chapter 19   Sweet Revenge

Everybody was in the parking lot when Whitey and I arrived. The four guys from the van, Perk, Reggie and Cye. Reggie got us together and started his speech. "While we took a day to relax these guys have been working. I had them keep an eye on this JJ or John Jr. He have been staked out watching his operation in Inglewood. Perk reported that he usually watches his money. He is usually at the spot most of the day with two or three guys. He sends one out to lunch around three o'clock every day. Drug traffic is usually heavy. So our window of opportunity is slim. We have to get in and get out quick. I suggest if it's alright with you ladies that we hit two places at one time. That way they won't have time to communicate with other family members. We should hit John Jr. and Mike Gucci at the same time. Then we go to the parents and then get out of this city, one way or the other. What you ladies think?" "I think that's a good idea, Tee what you want to do."Cye asked. "I wanna go to John Jr." I said. Cye said she is going where ever I'm going. Perk opened the van door and there was an arsenal of weapons. There were guns different sizes mounted on the walls of the truck. There was automatic weapons and ammunition on the back walls. On the open doors were bullet proof vest and silencers. Perk told Cye and I to put on a vest. All the other guys already had their vests on. Reggie told everybody to put silencers on their weapons. That would buy us time because no one will hear the shootings. Reggie told us his plan then we went and cleaned the hotel rooms down. We wiped down all flat surfaces taking the sheets with us and emptying the waste baskets. We didn't leave any evidence or DNA that could be traced back to us. Reggie and Whitey went to take care of Mike Gucci as we made our way to Inglewood, California.

While we were making our way to Inglewood the two policemen was getting off the plan at LAX airport. They had left their car in a No Parking Zone. It was still there because of the police plates on them. They headed out the airport to their destination, Mike Gucci's office. They had some questions to ask him about his brothers. Reggie and Whitey just made it to the tenth floor of the office building. They checked the exits and remembered where they were. They reached the law offices of Mike Gucci and partners. The receptionist was very polite. "Yes Mr. Gucci is in, Can I tell him your name please" she asked. Whitey said "We are friends of the family." The receptionist turned around to go get Mr. Gucci and Whitey was right on her heels. When she reached the door Whitey pushed her in. Reggie came in behind him. "What's the meaning of" is all he could get out before Reggie shot him in the forehead. As the woman attempted to scream Whitey shot her in the back of her head. She fell to the nice plush white carpet blood quickly flowed on the carpet and it turned red. She just happened to be in the wrong place at the wrong time. They couldn't afford to leave any witnesses to identify them. Both guys had on gloves so they picked up the shell casings and walked out his office door.

Sarkis and Hal got off the elevator on the tenth floor. "I got to take a leak" Sarkis said heading the opposite direction of Mike Gucci's office. "I'll meet you in his office, I want to flirt with his fine secretary" Hal said as he walked toward the office. He saw the two well dress men come out of Mike Gucci's office. He didn't pay much attention to them until he looked down and noticed they had on gloves. Hal reached for his service revolver just as Whitey turned and fired a shot that caught him on his arm. Hal fell down to grab his extra gun on his ankle. Reggie let off three shots killing him instantly. Whitey walked over to the fallen policeman and snatched his badge from around his neck. Both Reggie and Whitey took off for the exit. They had to run down ten flights of stairs before the place would be swarming with cops. Sarkis came into the office and saw Hal lying there in a pool of blood. He drew his gun. "Hal" he yelled. Sarkis called 911 and yelled policeman down and blurted out the address. He walked in the office with his gun ready to fire and saw Mike Gucci and his secretary lying in a pool of blood. He ran out and looked at the elevator. Then he ran to the exits. He cautiously moved through the staircase looking for the shooter. Reggie and Whitey made it to the first floor. They wiped the sweat off their fore-heads and fixed their ties. They walked through the lobby nonchalant talking about the Los Angeles Lakers. When they got to the door four police men almost knocked them down. They pushed right pass them running up the stairs. Within two minutes the office building was on lock down. Reggie and Whitey walked back to their car which was parked two blocks away cautiously. They headed toward Inglewood.

Perk, Cye and myself was parked a half block away from the drug house of John Gucci Jr. We watched to see if we could find a way in other then just blasting our way in. That way we might have some casualties. We watched as dope fiend after dope fiend go in and out of the house. Suddenly I had an idea. I got out he car pulled my pants down past my belt buckle. I told Cye to get out and she pulled her blouse out and messed up her hair. I messed up mine and picked up some dirt off the ground and put it on my face. I mixed it up with some spit. Cye looked at me and did the same. We looked like two drug addicts looking to cop some dope. We walked up the block with Perk trailing us half a block away. The van was watching all of our move's ready for any hint of trouble. I spotted a dope fiend leaving the house. He had to past Cye and I on his route. "Hey bro, can you cop for us we'll make worth your while." I said rubbing my hand and scratching my nose. "They don't sell no dope in there, just crack" he said. "We know man we just had to much H, and we want to get some good stuff" Cye said. "Here I'll give you fifty dollars" Cye handed the guy fifty dollars. He tried to walk away. "We're going with you, we spending $200. You can get high with us, but we got to go with you." Cye said. "Yea, last time we did this we got ripped off." I said. The dope fiend looked at the money in his hand and thought about the five dollar rock he had in his pocket. He could get high with them then buy a $30 rock to take home. This was a win win for him. "Ok, girls let's go. These guys don't like new people but you lucky I grew up with the family." He said. "What family" I asked. The Gucci family they run all the drugs in Cali. I went to school with JJ, Dom and Chris Jr." he bragged. Cye looked at me and I just kept scratching my nose. We got to the door and I looked around and saw Perk walking up the walk way next door. He knocked and the door was opened. We walked in and the guy at the door had a shotgun. The other guy was by a kitchen door and I guessed that JJ was in the kitchen.

"Give me the money" the dope fiend said. I reached in my pocket and gave him two hundred dollar bills. The guy at the door was looking at my roll of hundred dollar bills. "What you girls do rob a trick?" he said laughing. "I'll stay here girl, you go with him to make sure he don't rip us off, it that ok cutey" I asked the man at the door. "That's cool you can keep me company" I watched as Cye disappeared in the kitchen with the dope fiend. The guys looked down on us like we were just a couple of dope fiend hoes. It's another case where males under estimate females. There was a knock at the door. At the same time Cye stumbled out the kitchen. The guy at the kitchen entrance was watching the door. When he saw Cye fall to the ground he tried to pick her up. When he reached down to pick her up he was met with a bullet in his stomach. The guy at the door turned around to open it when I pulled my gun out and put it to the back of his head. "Open the door." I said as stern as I could. He opened the door and Perk burst in with his gun out. The guy figured out what was going on and turned to run or warn John Jr. He felt a sting in his neck and tried to ignore the pain. He took two more steps and Perk's bullet caught him in the back on his right side. The bullet went straight through you could hear it hit the wall. He dropped dead on the spot. I ran over to Cye while Perk watched the door. "Where is John Jr." I asked. I walked past Cye to the kitchen. John Jr. was at the table slumped over with two bullets in both his eyes. The poor dope fiend was sitting there with a crack pipe in his hand. But he never got to use it. He had one bullet in his head. Now, I was really beginning to worry about Cye. It just seems she snaps in and out when she is near any Gucci family member. She must get some psychiatric help when we get back to Detroit. "Alright lets clean up and get out of here." Perk said. Perk picked up all the shell casings and left. Outside the guys in the van was redirecting traffic. The crack heads turned the corner when they saw the van and the guys. They looked like police officer's still had on their gear and scarfs. We got in the car and pulled off and the van followed us. I called Reggie to see if everything went smooth for them. He said he would meet us in East Los Angeles.

Back at the police precinct Sarkis was called to his captain's office. He screamed and yelled at Sarkis. Then he calmed down. "Sarkis look I know you are a good detective and I know you are hurting because your partner got killed. But I need you to trust me. What is going on?" he asked. "I don't know Capt" Sarkis said. "do you think it's a mob war?" he asked Sarkis. "I don't know Capt" Sarkis said. "We have gotten five bodies in the last couple of days and ironically you called them in. Not to mention I heard you was at the house were two drugs users were killed. I'm not stupid you need to let me know what's going on" Captain I really don't know" he said. "Why were you in Detroit? I got invoices for plane fares. If you caught up in this somehow, I'll have your badge your pension and your fucking wife. You are now on a three day leave. Internal affairs will be calling you tomorrow. The damn commissioner is calling for your head. Now get the fuck out my office." The captain said and held the door open for him and slammed it when he passed through. The sound brought the eyes of every police officer in the station in his direction. They knew he was a dirty cop and they somehow felt he was responsible for his partner's death. The whole city was on lock down. The police were everywhere trying to find a clue to the murders. They harassed everybody that had a police record. Sarkis had his own plan. He felt if he could crack the case he could clear his name and avenge his partner. He knew all about the Gucci family since he had been working for them for over ten years. He figured that if someone wanted the whole family dead they have to come to their parent's house. The parents and Chris Jr, Chris Gucci's only son was the last Gucci's alive. Sarkis decided he would stake out the parents home for a couple of days.

Chapter 20

Killing The Last of the Guccis and Leaving Town

We drove to East Los Angeles and got a hotel on the outskirts of the city. Cye communicated with Reggie and he met us in the parking lot. When he and Whitey got out of the BMW with suits on I almost melted. Whitey looked so good. I just ran up to him and hugged him. "You all right baby" I said. He hugged me so tight like he wasn't going to see me again. Reggie and Cye were hugged up. "Look can we take care of this business so you guys can get a room" Perk said laughing. Reggie broke free from Cye. He walked over to the van and opened the door. "Everybody put all the guns that have been used in this bag. Wipe them off first." He said. He took out a bag from the van and loaded his weapon in it. Whitney, Perk and I put our weapons in there.

Reggie was getting ready to close the bag when the other four from the van put their guns in the bag. I had forgotten they killed TJ for turning against the crew. "All California is swarming with cops. We need to lay low for at least a day." Whitey said. I don't want anybody to go further then walking distance. Perk you and Marv go bury these guns." Reggie said. "One more thing, this is our final stand. If anybody wants to pull out I won't be mad at you. You have earned your $125,000 dollars. This last fight is for the ladies. You can leave now and I'll meet you in Detroit." "I'm staying with you" Whitey said. Perk said "I'm staying." All the guys said they were in it until the end. It felt good inside to know that someone will go all the way for you. I looked at Cye with tears in my eyes. Cye understood and came over hugged me. We left the guys standing there and walked to the hotel up to my room. Cye and I haven't talked in about a week. So much has happened. When we got to the room I asked Cye does she think she has closure. She looked at me with tears in her eyes.

"My daddy would be proud of us knowing we didn't let this rest until the people responsible for their deaths payed for it." She cried on my shoulders as she said. "After tomorrow Daddy, mama and aunt Lolo's spirit can rest in peace." I hadn't thought about it like that, but she was right. Cye and I let all our tears out that night. The mourning for our parents was over. We talked like we use to for hours. This time we were talking about the future. I was getting excited knowing I was going to see my daughter. Cye wanted to mend things with her sister. We counted up the money we had in a safe deposit box from Cye's notebook. We had a cool five million two hundred thousand and seventy five dollars. She had it down to the dollar. We both laughed. I hadn't seen Cye look so happy in a long time. She told me that she hadn't seen me this happy in a long time. She also told me that she was pregnant with Reggie's child. "That's why you're glowing so much" I said. She just smiled. We talked until four in the morning when Whitey and Reggie came to the room.

I think all the guys were drinking at the bar together planning their next move. I looked at Whitey from the couch and smiled. I think I got a new man. I say I think because you know how we ladies think. We let a men get our body see our freaky side, let them enter our world. Shit they better be our man after that. Cye and Reggie was hugging and kissing on the couch so I pulled Whitey in the bedroom. I looked into his eyes and said. "I want to thank you for having my back. I want to be with you forever." He held me and kissed me on my fore head and said. "I will always have your back." Tears begin to feel my eyes and my heart opened up. I let Carl out closed that chapter and let Whitey into my heart forever. I cried as he held me and asked me if I was alright. I told him I am now. We laid on the bed. He put in a movie and I just snuggled up next to him. He whispered in my ear. I'm falling in love with you Teeka Love Sinclair." I just held him tight as I drifted off to sleep. I woke up the next morning took a long hot shower. I had some nervous tension in my stomach. Usually that always means something bad is going to happen. Reggie told all of us to meet at one o'clock. I watched Whitey sleep. He didn't have on any shirt and I liked the way his chest hairs were as straight as his natural hair. I woke Whitey up with kisses on his nipples. He scrummed like he thought he was dreaming. I tenderly kissed him on the inside on his chest gently pulling the hair on his chest with my teeth. I gave him tender bites on his nipple that started to arouse him. He put his hand on my head and rubbed my ears. I continued kissing his chest while pulling down his underwear. He was excited and his manhood gave me to approval to go on. I kissed the inside of his naval and ran my tongue straight down to the top of his now fully erect dick. He moaned as I kissed the side's every so gently, making sure not to put my mouth on the head. I ran my tongue down the back of his dick to his balls. I licked each one while my hand caressed the other. He laid back and turned his head from side to side in complete ecstasy. I opened his legs with my knees and kissed the bottom of his jewels. I ran my tongue up from the beginning of his nuts to the head of his dick. I was teasing him and he was enjoying it. I finally put his manhood in my mouth and took slow long strokes. He couldn't take it anymore. I felt his dick pulsating in my mouth. I licked faster waiting for his juices to fill my mouth and show him how much love I had for him. Just when he was about to burst he pulled me up. "What's wrong I'm not doing it right." I asked. I was a little annoyed that he stopped. He looked me straight in my eyes and said. "No man who is going to spend the rest of their life's with a woman wants to come in their mouth, then kiss them the next day. I want you around forever I won't degrade you like that. He hugged me and pulled me on top of him. I opened my robe and put his hard manhood inside of me. I moved up and down slowly. This was the best love making I ever had. He kissed my titties as I bounced up and down on him. I came hard and long as he let out his juices inside me. I felt his hotness engulf my insides searching out a place to nurture. I laid in his chest with him inside me. He held me so tight I felt so secure. I didn't want to leave the security of his arms. My phone rang about an hour later. It was Cye she said that we were suppose to met the guys in the parking lot at one o'clock. We got up took a shower together and got dressed. When we got down stairs everybody was waiting on us. They all laughed and clapped. Whitey and I just smiled. Reggie gave us instructions and we all put on our game face. We loaded up our arsenal and headed to an exclusive neighborhood of Los Angeles.

    Sarkis was still camped out by the Gucci's parents home. He had been there for a couple of days. He was beginning to think that he was on the wrong trail. He started his car and went to get some coffee and donuts. This will be his last day he told himself. When he got up the block he noticed a black BMW pass him. He looked at it and kept going.

He turned at the next corner not noticing the black van go right pass him. Sarkis pulled up to the donut shop as Reggie and Whitey was pulling up to the large house. The neighborhood was filled mostly with older people out cutting there grass of working in there garden. Whitey walked to the door as Reggie and Perk went around the back. Whitey rang the door bell. A large man answered he looked like he use to be one of the goodfellows back in the day. Whitey should him his badge. The guy looked at it making sure it was authentic. He let him in. Whitey asked if he could speak to Mr. and Mrs. Gucci. "What precinct you from" the man asked. "I'm with homicide downtown" Whitey answered. "I use to work in Compton" the man said. He was trying=to intimidate Whitey. "Is Mr. and Mrs. Gucci here? I really need to talk to them." Whitey said watching every move the man made. Finally he said "they are up stairs you wait here" "You got a restroom" Whitey asked. "It's been a long drive and I have to piss." The man looked at Whitey then said "it's in the back by the kitchen." He didn't want Whitey to use the main bathroom up the hall. The man then headed upstairs to get the Gucci's and Whitey went through the kitchen. He looked for and found the back door. He let Perk and Reggie in and went back in the front foyer to wait for the Gucci's to come down. By the time the large man and Mr. and Mrs. Gucci came down the stairs Whitey had on his face mask. The bodyguard reached for his gun as Perk and Reggie became visible. "I wouldn't do that" Perk yelled. He still tried to pull his gun out. The first bullet from Reggie caught him in the chest. Whiteys bullet hit him in his arm where he was reaching for his gun. Perk's deadly bullet hit him left side of his temple and went right though his brain. Blood and brain splattered on the wall. He fell down the rest of the stairs. Dead before he hit the bottom stair. Mrs. Gucci started yelling and holding her chest. Mr. Gucci held his wife as the blood rushed to her brain. Her heart stopped beating and her eyes roled to the back of her head. "Help my wife" he said. She fell down the rest of the stairs almost landing on top of the bodyguard. Perk walked to the door and let Cye and I in. We walked over to the foyer and looked at the old man. He was crying "please help my wife" he pleaded. Tears were flowing down his face as he tried to give his wife mouth to mouth resuscitation. "Please help me" he said between tears. Cye and I looked at each other with tears in our eyes. I felt that this was enough we had gotten our revenge. Cye must have had the same thoughts. She had her gun in her hand then she put it down to her side. "Please, please" the man begged. He looked at his wife dead in his arms blue in the face and cold. He kissed her on the lips "I love you, Lucinda" he said as he cried. He looked up at Reggie and Whitey "Please kill me, I don't want to live any more she was my everything. I can't go on without her, please kill me." He begged. Cye looked at me tears rolling down her face. "I'm done sister, this is enough for me. I want to start the healing process." She said. Everybody looked at me for the final answer. Whitey and Reggie had their guns ready to end this man's life. I looked at Cye her eyes told me it was over. I just shook my head no to Reggie and Whitey. I turned around to leave as we heard sirens in the distant. Perk said "We need to go." Reggie and Whitey ran to the door and looked out. We got to roll out of" here Reggie said. Cye was standing off to the side wiping her face with tissue. The old man reached for the bodyguard's gun and pointed it at my back. Bang, bang caused us all to turn around as Cye was unloading her automatic weapon in the man's body. She didn't stop firing until I came and got the gun out of her hand. She still was pulling the trigger even though there were no bullets in the gun. "Thank you Cye" I said after I took the gun out of her hand. "Let's go" Perk said as he opened the door. Two gun shots went off and Perk fell back in the house. We then heard a lot of shots being fired. We knew it was the guys in the van. Reggie grabbed Cye and said come on. Whitney snatched my arm and headed for the kitchen. He said "Wait a minute." He went back to the foyer and dropped the police badge he had after he wiped it off. Perk followed us out. He was bleeding. We walked through three or four backyards and walked out front just as more police was arriving. Perk got in our car and Reggie and Whitey got in theirs. He always said they will stop two men before two women. We pulled off and we could see in our rear view mirror the guys in the van. They had the entrance blocked with the van and they were on each side firing at the police. It looked like something out of a movie. Reggie's car was noticed by a police cruiser coming in that direction. They turned around and gave pursuit. Cye drove down the next block. She was driving fast. "Slow down girl" I said. Just as I said it Sarkis was coming from the coffee shop. He looked at me and Cye as he passed us. Then he noticed Perk slumped in the back seat. His police scanner was dispatching SWAT teams. His police instincts kicked in. He spun around and put the siren on. Shit Cye said as she put her foot on the gas. Put your seat belt on she yelled. I put my belt on and turned around to see

Perk lying in the back seat. I think he was dead for losing so much blood. Cye turned corner after corner doing ninety miles an hour. The police was a block behind. Cye acted like she knew the area because she was losing them. Or either she had a destination. After a couple of miles I could hear more sirens. I thought to myself. If I gotta go out, this is the way I want it. I pulled my guns out and made sure I had bullets in both of them. I had two clips in my vest and one inside each gun. Somebody is leaving here with me. I thought to myself. While looking at my guns I didn't notice where Cye was going. I looked up to see that she had stopped after pulling into some garage. I could hear the police sirens speeding pass us. "Look, Teeka both of us don't have to die. You have your daughter Carletha to live for." she said. "No, you have your new baby and Reggie to live for. I'm not going to leave you."I said. "Teeka I love you and want to give my life for yours." "Cye I've been so proud of you and how you fought back for your life. I want you to enjoy the rest of your life." I said. "I'm not leaving you Cyrisa." "Teeka we've avenged our parents lives and now they can rest in peace. I want to join them." she said. "If you go I'm going too." We sat there holding each other saying our last goodbyes. The police sirens were coming back our way. She looked at me and said I love you. She pulled off and I cocked my gun ready to go out in a blaze of bullets. She suddenly stopped. The police sirens were getting closer maybe a block away. "What's wrong" I asked. "I need some more ammunition." She said. My gun clips are in the car trunk grab them right quick." I sprung the door open and headed for the trunk that Cye had popped open. I was looking in the trunk for the clips when Cye burned rubber and speed off. "Cye no" I cried. I stood there with my gun in my hand yelling "Cye please don't leave me." I ran to the entrance and watched Cye flying up the block with six police cars following her. Their sirens were blaring. I could hear the tire's of the cars burning the streets while turning the corners. As the sirens were fading I heard gun shots and then a large crash. I dropped to the sidewalk and cried. After a few minutes I called Reggie to see if they made it. The phone just rang and rang. I cried for Whitey. Sad I didn't get the opportunity to really love him. I dialed the phone again and again.

THE END

Discussion Questions:

1) Did Cye and Teeka get Revenge?

2) What happen to the two policemen?

3) Will Cye and Reggie Survive?

4) Should Whitey and Teeka become an item?

5) Are there any Gucci's left?

6) Will Dom's kid grow up and want revenge?

7) Did Cye get away.

Other books by Mark Saint Cyr

Mama Raised A Killer I

Books Coming out:

Mama Raised a Killer III "The Finally"

Coming out September 2010

Mama raised a Killer IV "The second Generation"

Coming out October 2010

Mama Raised A Killer II

TO ORDER BOOKS BY

MARK SAINT CYR

CONTACT US AT:

ATG TECHNOLOGIES & PUBLISHING

P O BOX 40422

REDFORD, MICHIGAN 48240

atgsmith@att.net

mrkii@att.net

visit our social web-site

atgcentral.com

a division of
Atg Technologies and Filmworks, LLC

Mark Saint Cyr

Mama Raised A Killer II